BEAU

Sue Brown

BEARYTALES #2

Copyright ©2023 Sue Brown

Published by One Hat Press
Cover design by Pippa Wood
Formatting by Format4U/Clare London

When a gruff Daddy thinks he's an ugly duckling, it takes a special boy to show him that he's a beau bear.

Damien has known his whole life that he was the ugly duckling of the seven Brenner brothers. But as a big Daddy bear, it didn't matter until Vinny comes into his life.

Another boy rescued from Kingdom Mountain Theme Park, Vinny is too young and too beautiful for an old bear like Damien. The age gap is too much. He needs a younger, gorgeous Daddy to take care of him.

Try telling Vinny that. He wants Damien to be his Daddy, and he's not going to accept no for an answer. He's sure he can out-stubborn Damien, with a little help from Damien's family.

Who is going to win this battle of wills?

Can Damien ignore his heart's desire and persuade Vinny he needs a fresh start away from the mountain and away from him? Or will Vinny finally persuade Damien that the only place he wants to be is in the arms of his beau bear?

All Rights Are Reserved. No part of this book may be used or reproduced in any manner whatsoever without written permission, except in the case of brief quotations embodied in critical articles and reviews.

This book is a work of fiction. While reference might be made to actual historical events or existing locations, the names, characters, places and incidents are either the product of the author's imagination or are used fictitiously, and any resemblance to actual persons, living or dead, business establishments, events, or locales is entirely coincidental.

Contents

Chapter 1

Damien age 12

Damien rushed into the cabin, smiling as he heard his mother cooing at her new-born. All his chores done, it was his turn to cuddle his baby brother. The rest of his brothers laughed at him, but they all knew the oldest of the Brenner boys loved them fiercely and protectively, and the latest addition to the Brenner household was no exception. At school, they'd told him that baby birds followed their mother because she was the first face they saw. He couldn't be the first face of course, because his mom and dad were their parents, but he firmly believed in imprinting on his baby brothers as soon as possible. It seemed to work too. They followed him all the time.

Damien loved his six brothers, but as the oldest, a lot of the responsibility for looking after the older boys fell on him, while his mom took care of the little ones. With his dad working on their Christmas tree farm all the time, he was more like a father-figure to them. He hoped, maybe, his mom and dad would stop asking the stork to bring them a girl. It was obvious the bird was a boy stork who only brought boys.

But then he heard another woman speak and grimaced. It was their neighbor. New babies always brought lots of people to the cabin. Damien couldn't understand why. By the seventh boy he'd have thought the novelty would have worn off, but they still flocked to the cabin.

"Oh Mollie, the little one is gorgeous. What are you going to call him?"

In Damien's opinion, some visitors were more welcome than others. He didn't like old Mrs. Viner. She was always trying to interfere in the way his mom did everything from bringing up the kids to cooking the dinner. His dad said it was because her husband and son ignored her. Her son had just taken a job in the Kingdom Mountain Theme Park just up the mountain. Mrs. Viner was very proud of him. He got to wear a green coat, and she showed everyone a photo of him in his uniform. But she was always complaining he never visited her, and he was only just up the mountain road.

"His name is Gregory, but Jake calls him Gruff." His mom sounded weary. "They all call him Gruff now."

"Little Gruff," Mrs. Viner chuckled. "What's he? Number seven?"

Damien's mom sighed. "Yes, but that's all now. I've told Jimmy I've had enough. I'm just thankful I have Damien to help me."

Damien wrinkled his nose at Mrs. Viner's derisive hum. She was nasty, but no matter how often he told his mom, she just told him not to be rude. He had to respect Mrs. Viner.

"Well, your Damien has to be good for something. He's never going to be a looker. Your boys certainly improved the more you had. This one is as cute as a button."

Damien waited for his mom to defend him, to say he was beautiful or something. But all she said was "He's a young and growing lad. He's got time to improve."

Mrs. Viner sniffed. "He's certainly an ugly duckling compared to this little man. He won't be handsome enough to become a green coat like *my* Eddie."

"We need Damien to work on the farm," his mom said mildly. "The theme park can do without his help."

Damien flinched as they discussed his future like he had no say in the matter. He'd always wanted to get off the mountain and travel the world. He had a huge picture of the world pinned up in his bedroom, and he entertained his little brothers by getting them to pick a place on the map and telling them all about the country.

"Let's hope he finds a girl who doesn't care that he's not a looker," Mrs. Viner said.

"Looks aren't everything. Damien's got a kind heart," Damien's mom protested.

Damien rocked back on his heels. He was consumed with hatred for Mrs. Viner, but the biggest betrayal was his mom. Damien was crushed by his mom's lack of support. She thought he was ugly. He bit his lip against the sudden tears in his eyes. He wouldn't cry. He was a big boy now. Crying was for little kids. He wiped at his eyes impatiently. It didn't matter that he wasn't handsome. He was never going to get married, and he didn't like girls anyway. They had cooties.

He backed away from the kitchen, needing to find somewhere to hide. He needed time to get over the hurt in his heart at his mother's betrayal. He'd hide at the woodshed. No one would follow him there.

Before he could run away, a cry went up from the main room.

"Damie, I lost my Legos." PJ ran toward him, his face smeared with dirt and tears. "They were here and now they're gone."

Damien opened his mouth to yell that he didn't care about Legos, but then he saw PJ's expression and his heart melted as it always did where his brothers were concerned.

"We put them away last night, remember? So Mom wouldn't trip over them and drop little Gruff."

"But my spaceship was going to Mars," PJ wailed.

Damien *oofed,* staggering back as PJ ran into him. At six years old, PJ was already tall and broad enough to leave bruises.

"Easy, buddy." At least Damien could explain away the tears now. "Your spaceship is in one piece. Let's take the Legos box upstairs and you can play with them in my bedroom."

PJ nodded, all smiles now. "You can play with me, but not Jakey, cos he breaks things."

Jake was two. He broke a lot of things. Damien

spent a lot of time stopping the older brothers from yelling at Jake.

"Let's sneak up," Damien suggested.

PJ grinned and tip-toed to the stairs.

Damien retrieved the Legos box from the playroom and followed PJ up the stairs. He caught sight of himself in the big mirror at the top of the stairs. Dark, floppy hair, square jaw, blue eyes. He looked like a younger version of his father. Damien frowned. His mom loved his dad despite that. Damien took a deep breath. It didn't matter what he looked like. He still didn't like girls.

Vinny, age 17

The cane hit him over and over, the searing pain flaring along the weal, dominating his body and soul. Vinny couldn't speak, couldn't breathe. All he could see was the green coat holding him so he couldn't escape.

Vinny sighed and pushed away the unhappy memories as he faced yet another pile of potatoes he had to peel. He thought he'd gotten away from kitchen duty, but in a household of seven huge men, he discovered just how much they ate. Vinny was grateful for being rescued from the Kingdom Mountain theme park, along with all the other orphans, but sometimes he felt like Cinderella, stuck in the kitchen, while everybody else went off to the ball. He was small and skinny compared to the huge Brenner bears. They weren't really bears but Vinny was convinced there had been a grizzly or two somewhere in their ancestry.

He was a good cook, and they were all very appreciative of the dinners he put in front of them, but he really hated peeling potatoes. It didn't escape his notice that Lyle, his friend from the theme park, found every excuse not to help him. He'd understood while Lyle's sprained wrist recovered. Lyle's Daddy had thrown him onto the road from a moving vehicle as it went over the side of a mountain. Both Lyle and his Daddy had been lucky to survive. But Lyle's wrist was fine now, and he was a better cook than Vinny. When Vinny had complained about it however, Lyle had said that once Vinny was eighteen, he didn't have to stay in the Brenner household. Neat deflection. He didn't mention the potatoes at all.

The idea of going into the big wide world made him break out into a cold sweat. He'd never lived anywhere except locked up in the Kingdom Mountain theme park. Just the thought of going off the mountain kept him awake at night, but he kept that to himself. He didn't want to be a burden to the Brenners. Not once had Damien—they—ever said he was welcome to stay and become family as Lyle had. He kept hoping but it never happened. Instead, potatoes and more potatoes.

Vinny sighed again and picked up the first potato.

"Where's Grumpy?" PJ asked as he walked into the kitchen.

Vinny frowned at the peeler in his hand, knowing PJ was talking about his eldest brother. He hated the way all the brothers talked about Damien. In Vinny's eyes, Damien was his hero and he had to bite back the angry words he wanted to say to PJ. He was a guest in their house. No, not even a guest. Guests were invited. He was more of a refugee, hiding from green coats, the evil men who ran the theme park, until he was eighteen and had no chance of being disappeared. All the orphans knew 'disappeared' was a euphemism for killed. The alternative was just as horrific. Some boys were turned into sex slaves for the green coats.

"I think *Damien* is chopping logs for the fires," Vinny said pointedly.

PJ grunted. "Go tell him I need to talk to him, okay?"

Vinny's heart gave a leap as it always did at being able to talk to Damien. He had no control over himself around the eldest of the Brenner brothers. His heart and dick were firmly Damien's, even if the man seemed determined to ignore him.

He looked up to see PJ eyeing him shrewdly. He flushed, realizing his crush on Damien was well known by the family. "I've got to peel potatoes. You know where he is. You could just go and find him yourself."

"You mean to say you don't want to talk to my big brother?"

PJ was a horrendous tease. Vinny wasn't going to get away with not finding Damien. PJ lived to annoy his eldest brother. After four weeks of living in the Brenner household he knew all the tensions between the brothers. As the youngest, Gruff tended to get most of the teasing, but that had eased as he was the only one in a settled relationship. Now Damien was the current target. Vinny didn't like the way they tormented Damien, but he seemed to be oblivious to it.

PJ sniffed appreciatively as he lifted the lid to the pan full of hot chocolate that always lived on the stovetop. "Off you go. Chop chop."

Vinny knew PJ just wanted to drink all the hot chocolate in the pan. PJ was the worst for emptying the rich chocolaty goodness and not replacing it. Vinny muttered under his breath as he stamped into his boots and put on his jacket and hat. He knew better than to curse out loud now. Each swear word cost a dollar in the Brenner household, and as he had no money, Damien had to pay for him. He didn't want to give Damien any reason to be cross and make him leave. Vinny was the only one who'd been lucky enough to be brought into the Brenner household after Lyle and the brothers rescued the orphans.

Vinny didn't mind going to find Damien. He never minded going to find the big gruff Daddy bear. But he knew the potatoes would still be waiting for him when he got back.

He crunched through the snow towards the yard. It was strange living on the Christmas tree farm. The surroundings were the same, yet his small world had turned upside down. He had spent almost his entire life in the Kingdom Mountain theme park, which was just up the mountain. Vinny didn't remember his parents or his home. His mom and dad had died too young for him to have any memories before the theme park. At least that's what the green coats told him.

Despite the teasing between the brothers, they had all been so kind to him. He had his own bedroom for the first time in his life. Sometimes he felt if he blinked, he would be back in the dorm room sharing with nineteen other boys, his days filled with endless chores as they kept the theme park running. All the visitors were unaware of the atrocities meted out to the boys. He used to watch the moms and dads and kids having fun, and then they'd go home, never knowing about the children left behind.

Vinny knew he'd never set foot in another theme park again. He knew what happened behind the scenes. The brothers had tried to tell him not all theme parks were like that. Vinny asked how did they know? None of them could answer and Lyle just kept quiet.

Thwack! Thwack!

Vinny stopped, his mouth dry and cock hard, as he watched Damien use the axe, splitting the logs. He had obviously gotten hot and had stripped down to his undershirt, despite the chill wind. Watching Damien chop logs was like watching art in motion. All rippling muscle and powerful masculinity. From his hiding place in the trees, Vinny feasted on the sight, his mouth watering at the powerful muscles covered in a sheen of sweat, the curls of dark hair peeking over the top of the undershirt.

The green coats had been powerful too. They used their power to hurt the boys in their care. In the first days of living with the brothers, Vinny had waited for Damien to hurt his younger siblings, but he never had, not once. His heart was as big as his body. Damien would lay down his life for his family. Vinny sighed. Damien was stunning inside and out, and Vinny wanted nothing more than to kneel at his feet for the rest of his life. It was just a shame Damien didn't see it.

As Damien swung the axe up again, Vinny shifted to get a better view and trod on an old, dry stick which snapped loudly. Damien paused, the axe poised, and Vinny saw the familiar pinched expression replace the relaxed happiness he'd worn a moment before. Vinny cursed under his breath for destroying the moment that Damien could relax and be himself.

Vinny moved into the clearing so Damien could see him. "Hi."

He saw a flare of something in Damien's eyes. No matter how hard Damien tried to hide it, Vinny knew that Damien wanted him, but just as quickly Damien shuttered his expression.

"Are you all right, Vinny?"

Always the first question.

Vinny wondered what would happen if he said no. But he wouldn't play games with Damien. He cared about him too much even if he was as frustrated as hell.

"I'm fine. PJ wants to talk to you."

Damien huffed and Vinny held back a grin. His relationship with his middle sibling was always fractious. PJ seemed to love pushing his last nerve.

"He didn't think to walk here and tell me himself?" Damien muttered.

"He was more interested in the contents of the pan on the stovetop," Vinny said in a confiding tone.

Damien grunted. It wasn't like that was news. Where PJ was concerned, his stomach always came first. But Vinny wasn't interested in PJ. There was only one brother who held his attention, and he was the big, stern bear standing in front of him. He edged closer to Damien, smiling at him.

"You know I'm eighteen next week," Vinny said.

Damien's wide mouth curved into a smile. "You have told me...once or twice."

Vinny couldn't help his smirk. Well, yeah, of course he'd been *hinting* at his impending age. Just hinting, nothing more. Once he reached eighteen there would be no reason Damien couldn't claim Vinny as his.

"Once it's your birthday you can leave here safely. You've got no chance of being disappeared," Damien said.

Vinny stared at him, his heart sinking. Was Damien really that oblivious to how Vinny felt about him? The last thing he wanted was to leave here. He knew that once he reached his eighteenth birthday any remaining green coats wouldn't be interested in him. But they were safely in jail. They couldn't disappear him. Vinny had once believed the lie that the boys went out into the world and found jobs and homes. But the truth was far more sinister. They were drugged and left to die in the woods surrounded the cabin. The brothers had found bodies over the years, believing the young men to be hikers lost in the woods. Lyle had been the first to survive and only because Gruff had brought him back to cabin to keep him away from predators.

The cabin represented safety now, yes, but Vinny wanted it to be his home, with Damien. He wanted what Lyle had, a Daddy Bear who loved him.

Chapter 2

Damien

The snap of the wood told Damien he wasn't alone. He sighed inwardly. All he wanted was an hour to himself. An hour where he didn't watch what he had to say. Time where he could daydream about Vinny being on his lap, teaching him to read and write because none of the Kingdom boys had any education. Time where he could feed Vinny and bathe him and whisper in his ear that no one would ever hurt him again. But making Vinny his was a forlorn hope, just like his dream of traveling the world. One to be forgotten as quickly as possible.

Damien looked up, wondering which one of his brothers was here to annoy him. As Vinny strolled into the clearing, Damien wondered what he'd done in a previous life to deserve this torment. Vinny was young and beautiful and slender. Not a sweet boy like Lyle. He was more wary than Gruff's boy. Less trusting maybe. But feisty and determined to make the most of his new life. He'd been scared of Damien when he'd first met him, but Damien had earned his trust.

Vinny's smile, a touch apologetic, seemed to

light up the yard. Damien couldn't drag his gaze away from him. Vinny was a foot shorter than him, slim and vibrant, his eyes the greenest Damien had seen, and his long dark hair thick and luscious. Vinny talked about cutting it, but Damien wanted to forbid him. Vinny was perfect as he was. He wanted to rake his fingers through it and drag Vinny toward him. But he didn't have the authority to do that.

Damien snorted as Vinny relayed PJ's message. So typical of his lazy brother not to shift his ass and find Damien himself. Did PJ really want to talk to him or did he want to torment Damien with Vinny? Damien knew his crush—did people even use that term anymore—was not unnoticed by his brothers. They all knew each other too well to be able to hide things. And PJ loved using Vinny to press Damien's buttons. He wouldn't be able to do it when Vinny left the farm to discover new adventures.

"Have you decided what you want to do first on your birthday?" Damien asked.

"You."

Damien's jaw dropped open at Vinny's immediate response. He stared at the boy. Did he really just hear that? "What?"

"You asked what I wanted to do, and that's you," Vinny said, as if Damien were a child who needed a patient explanation.

"You can't...I can't..." Damien spluttered.

Vinny held his head high and defiant, but the sheen in his eyes was hard to miss. "I'll be eighteen. Not a kid anymore."

"Vinny, we've been through this. I'm forty, you're seventeen."

"Eighteen," Vinny snapped.

"Whatever. I'm too old for you."

"That's not true. Lyle's only just eighteen."

"And Gruff is only twenty-eight. You know he's my youngest brother and I'm twelve years older than him," Damien pointed out. "And even he feels the age gap sometimes."

"Damien, please." Vinny twisted his hands around the old coat he was wearing.

Vinny had been as excited as Lyle to be given the worn and faded clothes from when the brothers were young. He had spent years in the Kingdom Mountain green uniform, and he refused to wear anything green. This coat had been one of Damien's originally. Damien noticed Vinny preferred to wear Damien's clothes even though they were the most well-worn, having been handed down through seven boys.

"You know I don't care about the age gap. I just care about you," Vinny insisted, suddenly looking very young and vulnerable. "Don't you like me, Dad—Damien."

Damien sighed and put down the axe. He couldn't bear to see Vinny look as scared and fearful as he had when Damien had first met him. He held out his arms and Vinny ran into them hard. Damien wrapped his arms around the boy and rested his chin on Vinny's head.

Mistake.

Big mistake.

Damien was now holding the boy he loved in

his arms. What was he thinking?

Vinny pressed into Damien, wriggling like an eager puppy, and sighed happily as he rested his head on Damien's chest. He didn't seem to care that Damien was hot and sweaty or notice that the big guy was having a freak-out above him.

Damien looked down at the boy's glossy hair, all soft and just right for him to press a kiss into it. No, he had to stay strong. He had to be the adult in the relationship and make Vinny see that Damien wasn't the right Daddy for him. But he never wanted to let the boy go.

"I like you, Vinny," he said quietly. 'Like' was a pale comparison of what he really felt about the boy. But he had to do the right thing for both their sakes. "But I'm not the right man for you."

Vinny raised his head, and his expression was fierce. "You keep saying that, and I'm telling you you're wrong. You're all I've ever wanted in a Daddy."

Damien let his arms fall away and stepped back. Vinny looked as crushed as a boy could look, but also fucking angry too. Good, he wanted Vinny to keep that fire in his belly. That would make it easier for when he eventually left them. It was fire that had kept these boys alive for so long.

"I hate you," Vinny spat, his green eyes full of tears, and turned on his heel to run away.

Damien watched Vinny disappear through the trees and sighed, knowing he'd fucked up again. For the right reasons, but knowing he'd hurt the boy and that's the last thing he wanted to do. How many more times would Vinny accept rejection before he never came back. The day that happened would crush Damien's heart, but it was for the best. He wasn't the right guy for the vibrant young man. At forty, the age gap loomed between them. Vinny needed a Daddy who was young and beautiful, just like him. Maybe one of his younger brothers, like Jake. Vinny didn't deserve the ugly duckling of the family.

Damien picked up the axe and returned to splitting the logs. If PJ wanted to talk to him, he could come find Damien himself. Damien would be here, with his heart breaking in pieces as if it were the one under the axe.

Vinny

Vinny stomped into the cabin, the door giving a loud crack as it slammed back and hit the wall. The conversation died in the kitchen as the four men sitting at the table turned to look at him.

"Uh, Vinny. Are you all right?" Gruff asked.

"I'm fine," Vinny snarled as he stalked out of the kitchen to the stairs.

He was just peachy at being rejected again.

"What the hell's wrong with the boy?" That was Harry, the only redhead of the family.

"I imagine big brother said no again," PJ said.

Vinny heard their mocking laughter. He clenched his jaw. So they found his heartbreak fucking funny, did they? Vinny was done. He was out of this place. He could hitchhike down the mountain road and be away before anyone noticed. If Damien didn't want him, Vinny would take his chances in the big wide world.

But he paused on the bottom step when he heard someone say, "I'll talk to Vinny. It's upsetting him." This voice was quieter, not so deep as the others. Lyle always had Vinny's back.

"Who are you talking about now? Damien or Vinny?" PJ said, making Vinny grit his teeth. "The kid's gotta do the potatoes."

"Peel the potatoes yourself," Gruff said irritably. "Vinny is our guest, not our slave."

Lyle gave a long sigh. "Either. Both. This delay is killing them."

Vinny blinked, trying to process the two separate threads of the conversation.

"Got to give it to Damien," Gruff said. "I didn't think he'd hold out. The boy's been throwing himself at Damien since the first moment he saw him."

PJ snorted a laugh. "If Damien doesn't want to take the boy in hand, I'll do it. I'm happy to tap that tight ass."

Never in a million years. Vinny was sure of that. Not if PJ was the last Daddy on earth.

"You lay one finger on Vinny, and you'll be eating your teeth," Damien snarled, the door slamming for the second time in as many minutes. "No one touches him. He's mi—"

Mine? Is that what Damien had been going to say? Despite his anger, Vinny couldn't help thrilling to the way Damien claimed him, at least to his brothers. He'd tell everyone that Vinny was his. Except Vinny himself. It was so frustrating.

"Then tell him that," Gruff said. "How's he

supposed to know if you don't tell him he's loved."

"I can't." Vinny heard the anguish in Damien's voice. "He's underage. It's not right."

"He's gonna be eighteen next week, bro," PJ said.

"I'm too old for him."

Vinny rolled his eyes. What did he have to do to convince Damien he didn't care?

"Vinny doesn't think so," Lyle said. "He wants you."

Vinny was really lucky to have a friend like Lyle. Once the shyest of boys, he was now loved and protected by his Daddy, and it showed in his new-found confidence. That's what Vinny wanted for himself. Was that so wrong?

"Vinny doesn't know what he wants," Damien said. "He needs someone young and beautiful to take care of him."

Vinny blinked. Beautiful? Where had that come from?

"Not to labor the point," Gruff said, "but my boy is pointing out the obvious. He doesn't want young and beautiful. For whatever reason, the kid wants you."

Vinny held his breath as he waited for Damien to respond.

"No, I'm not the one for him. I know that."

"Then why do you look so miserable, Damien?" Lyle asked softly.

The only response was the door slamming.

There was silence for a moment.

"Grumpy's got it bad for the kid," PJ said finally.

"Yeah," Harry agreed. "But you know what he's like. He's never gonna think he's good enough for anyone."

"I'll take the kid—"

PJ stopped under a hail of "Shut the fuck up," from the others.

"A dollar from all of you," PJ said, and Vinny heard the rattle of coins.

Lyle really had come out of his shell if he was brave enough to curse at PJ.

Still sitting on his perch on the stairs, Vinny shuddered. There was only one Daddy he was interested in, and it wasn't PJ.

He wasn't surprised when Lyle came to find him.

"You heard all that?" Lyle asked.

Vinny nodded.

"Damien's being an idiot."

Vinny couldn't help smiling at his friend's strident declaration. "You know that, and I know that." The smile faded away as Vinny hugged himself, feeling as if he were going to fly apart. Damien kept him grounded. "Why doesn't he want me, Lyle? I know he likes me."

Lyle sighed as he sat down next to Vinny and wrapped an arm around his shoulders, encouraging Vinny to rest his head on Lyle's shoulder. It was good and familiar, but Vinny really wanted Damien to be the one holding him.

"He more than likes you. But he's scared."

"Of me?"

"Of getting his heart broken again."

Vinny felt a cold hand close around his heart.

20

"He was in love with someone else?"

Lyle shook his head, and the clutch eased a fraction. "It's Damien's story to tell. He's being an idiot. But don't give up on him, Vinny. You just have to convince him otherwise."

"How do I do that?" Vinny asked, his voice very small.

Lyle held him closer. "Just love him, Vinny. Your Daddy needs you."

Chapter 3

Damien

Two days later Damien was sick of lurking in the barn and if he cut any more logs, he'd have to start on the Christmas trees which would defeat the point of the farm.

"When are you gonna quit hiding from him?" Gruff asked from the doorway.

Damien glowered at him. "I'm not hiding."

"You are," Gruff said, his voice almost pitying. "You know it, we know it, and more to the point, he knows it. And you're hurting him."

Damien hated the pity he saw in Gruff's eyes, and he hated the thought he was causing Vinny a second of pain.

"I'm not. I'm trying to help him."

"Why won't you accept him as your boy?"

"He needs—"

"He needs the man who loves him," Gruff said. "What are you? A Daddy or a mouse?"

Damien frowned. "That doesn't make sense."

"Who cares. You know what I mean. You're a Daddy. Behave like one." Gruff came over and squeezed Damien's shoulder. "Come back to the house, Damien. We all miss you."

Damien slumped against Gruff. "Am I really being an idiot?"

"You know you are."

"But—"

"No buts. You've got a boy to look after."

Damien turned to look at Gruff. "You're my little brother. When did you get to tell me what to do?"

"When you quit behaving like my big brother. Vinny thinks you're a hero. It's time you behaved like one."

Ouch!

But Gruff was right. He *was* being an idiot.

"I can't...with him...not yet."

Damien stumbled over the words, but Gruff nodded. "You're right. Wait until his birthday. It doesn't do a boy any harm to wait a while to get what he wants."

"You're talking as if he's the one in charge of the relationship."

Gruff rolled his eyes. "Oh, big brother. You've got a lot to learn about having a boy of your own."

Damien thought about being offended but Gruff didn't give him a chance, manhandling him out of the barn and toward the house.

"You know it's not just Vinny who needs you, Damien," Gruff said before they reached the cabin. "We all do. You're our big brother, the leader of the pack. When you go missing it's like we're without our anchor."

Damien stopped and studied him. "The others maybe. But not you. You've got a new anchor now."

Gruff beamed at him. "You see that?"

"I think I saw it the moment you walked into the house with him. Suddenly you weren't my kid brother anymore. You were Lyle's Daddy."

Gruff knocked him with his elbow. "I'll always be your kid brother. As for being someone's Daddy, I'd like to remind you from the second you met Vinny you held his hand and promised you would take care of him. He's waiting for you to make good on your promise."

"He needs a younger Daddy."

"He needs you," Gruff said pointedly. "Now step up or PJ will."

No!

Damien growled at him and Gruff nodded. "Yeah, that's what I mean."

Gruff shoved him up the stoop and into the cabin. Damien was getting damned tired of being shoved around as if Gruff worried he was going to bolt. Maybe he had a point.

"Damien, about time!" Jake yelled as they entered the kitchen.

They had other rooms they could sit in, but somehow, they always ended up in the kitchen.

"Move over, PJ," Brad grumbled.

The chorus of calls and yells almost overwhelmed Damien after the peace of the barn, but Damien found himself at the table in his usual place, with Vinny by his side. Damien tuned out his brothers and focused on Vinny, seeing the dark smudges under his eyes. It didn't take a rocket scientist to work out he was the reason Vinny hadn't been sleeping. "Are you sleeping all right?"

Vinny looked away. "No."

"You need to get your rest."

"I don't sleep well when you don't put me to bed," Vinny muttered.

Damien had done that each night since Vinny arrived at the cabin. Taking him to bed, undressing him, and tucking him in. Gruff was right. He'd let Vinny down.

He took one of Vinny's hands in both of his. "I'm sorry. I'll take you to bed tonight."

"Promise?"

"I promise," Damien assured him.

He didn't let go of Vinny's hand as he took a deep breath and looked around the table at his family. Lyle was sitting on Gruff's lap as usual. Damien caught Vinny's sideways hungry looks as he watched them. Vinny wanted what his friend had.

Damien sighed inwardly. Was he hurting them both by saying no? He was sure he was doing the right thing for Vinny, but it just seemed to be making them miserable.

At least he was back in the cabin again, and warm for what seemed to be the first time in days. Vinny shuffled his seat closer to Damien who didn't pull away. But Damien steadfastly refused to meet Gruff's gaze even if it was boring a hole into his cheek.

Lyle insisted everyone had chips and snacks along with large cups of hot chocolate with fluffy marshmallows. Damien fed Vinny the snacks, controlling a shiver when Vinny licked the salt from his fingers. He got a lot of eyebrow waggles for doing that. He ignored them all.

Damien wasn't sure when Vinny fell asleep. One minute he was laughing at something PJ said and the next he was laying in Damien's lap, snoring gently. Damien stroked his long hair, noting it was in need of a good brush. He'd been the one to brush Vinny's hair each morning, but the past couple of mornings, he'd deliberately gotten up before anyone was awake. It looked as if Vinny hadn't bothered brushing it at all.

He really needed to offer the boy a Brad special. Not only did Brad like blowing things up and writing poetry about it, but he was also a whizz with the clippers. He glanced around the table. The whole family could do with a trim; they were looking decidedly shaggy. The brothers had all had other things on their minds since rescuing a twink from certain death in the woods. Damien glanced at Lyle. He'd turned their sedate lives upside down.

"He's been so miserable," Harry said quietly, nodding down at the sleeping boy. "And crying when he thinks no one else can hear."

"He's not been the only one," Damien muttered, threading his fingers through Vinny's dark hair.

"What are you scared of, Damien? He adores you."

"Being the one left behind again."

Damien really hadn't meant to say that. He clamped his mouth shut against any more unwelcome utterances.

"You mean Mom and Dad?" Harry asked.

Damien didn't answer. He didn't need to. They knew how he felt.

"You can't tell the future. You can only enjoy the present. And letting this boy slip through your fingers because you're scared is a really stupid mistake."

Damien was starting to feel battered by all the brotherly advice. "Is this have a go at big brother day? Did I miss the memo?"

"Yes," Harry snapped. "I sent it out. You were hiding in the barn."

Damien supposed he asked for that.

He stayed at the table until the urge to hide again overcame him, but this time he picked up Vinny and carried him upstairs. Seven pairs of eyes followed him.

"Nosy bastards," he muttered, and made a mental note to put a dollar in the jar.

Vinny grumbled something incoherent and snuggled in closer to Damien.

"Shhh, boy, I've got you," Damien soothed.

Vinny roused enough to stand passively while Damien undressed him, then sat at on the bed while Damien sat behind him and brushed his hair until it was smooth, glossy, and tangle-free.

Damien coaxed him into bed. Vinny never bothered wearing pajamas. After a lifetime of sharing of a room with nineteen other boys, he wasn't self-conscious about his body, and he said he was so used to being cold, now he was in a comfortable bed he was almost too warm if he wore anything.

He caught Damien's hand as he turned away. "Don't hide in the barn tomorrow?"

"Things haven't changed," Damien said. "I still think I'm too old for you."

He saw the hurt in Vinny's eyes, but the boy nodded. "I know. You're wrong. And I'm gonna show you."

Damien gave him a wry grin. He had to give the boy props for persistence. "You think you can change my mind, huh?"

"If you don't disappear from me again."

"I won't hide away in the barn," Damien promised.

He was done hiding.

Vinny

Hunter's tawse hit him over and over, the pain dominating his body and soul. Vinny couldn't speak, couldn't breathe. All he could see was the green coat holding him so he couldn't escape. He focused on the man's clear blue eyes, cold and heartless, taking pleasure in his pain.

His body couldn't take any more. He was going to die in the tower, watching a man reveling in his death.

"Shh, boy, it's all right. I've got you. Hush now. It's all right."

Vinny struggled weakly, trying to get away but he was held fast, unable to move his arms. "Please stop. Please, no more. I can't take it."

"Vinny, it's Damien. I've got you. You're safe."

The pain in his chest loosened fractionally and Vinny gasped "Gonna die."

"You're safe, Vinny. They can't hurt you again. I promise. You're not going to die. It's Damien. Listen to my voice, Vinny. You're safe. I promise you."

Still lost in the terror of the nightmare, Vinny could hear the promises rumbled in his ear. He latched onto the one thing that made sense to him.

"Damien?"

"It's me. I've got you, boy. I won't let you go."

Vinny wasn't sure this was real or just his desperate fantasy after days of Damien avoiding him. Damien had apologized for that, but did he really mean it?

He listened to the *thump thump* beneath his ear, the comforting rhythm soothing him. As he came fully awake, he realized the sound was Damien's heartbeat and Damien's soft chest hair tickled his cheek. Vinny stayed there for a long time, unwilling to lose the comfort.

There was a soft knock at the door.

"Vinny?" Lyle sounded worried.

He shivered, not realizing Lyle had come in. He buried his face in the fur on Damien's chest.

Damien held him close and rocked him. "It's all right, Lyle. I've got him. Go back to bed."

"Okay. If you're sure. I could sit with him."

Vinny whimpered. Even though Lyle was his best friend and knew better than anyone why he suffered the nightmares, he couldn't face him at that moment.

"Come on, boy," Gruff said. "Damien can take care of Vinny."

He just wanted them to go. The weight of their concern was pressing down on him. It was a relief when he heard footsteps, then a door close.

"They've gone," Damien murmured and rocked him until Vinny was sleepy again.

He yawned and pressed his cheek against Damien's furry chest. When Vinny had bad dreams, Damien was there as he'd been from Vinny's first night in the cabin. No one else was allowed to comfort Vinny when he was upset. Vinny wondered if Damien found it easier to show his feelings in the dark.

"Are you ready to sleep?" Damien said.

Vinny wrapped his arms around Damien. "Don't leave me."

Damien sighed and Vinny found himself under the covers with Damien spooning around him. The narrow bed was barely big enough for the two of them. They slept like this every time Vinny had nightmares.

"Will you ever let me sleep in your bed?" he whispered, the darkness giving him confidence.

"Oh, baby boy, it wouldn't be a good idea."

Vinny scowled, hearing the yearning in Damien's voice. He wanted it as much as Vinny did. Why was he holding back?

"I think it would be a very good idea. And there would be more room."

Two men in a single bed was a squeeze, particularly when one of them was built like a mountain.

"If I let you into my bed, I'd never let you go." Damien's confession was almost a whisper.

"Would that be so wrong?" Vinny demanded.

The silence stretched on for an eternity.

"I'm not the right man for you," Damien said eventually.

Tears prickled Vinny's eyes. "You promised you'd take care of me."

Damien had pledged that at their first meeting and Vinny clung to that promise. The big, grim-faced man had scared him initially, then made him feel so safe.

"I'll never let anything happen to you," Damien said.

A tear rolled down Vinny's cheek. He knew Damien cared for him. So why did that sound like goodbye?

The knock at the door disturbed his uneasy sleep. Vinny rolled over, unsurprised to find his bed empty. Damien never stayed the night. He remembered murmuring a protest when Damien had gotten out of bed, but the big man had just kissed his forehead and told him to go back to sleep.

The door opened and Lyle smiled at him.

"Are you staying in bed all day?"

Vinny sat up and yawned. "What's the time?"

He'd not been impressed to discover the brothers got up at five in the morning and he was also expected to get up to prepare the breakfasts.

"Nearly ten o'clock."

Vinny stared at Lyle. "You're kidding."

"Nope. Damien said you didn't sleep so well after the past few days and to let you sleep in."

Vinny grimaced. "I had another nightmare too."

Lyle perched on the end of the bed and turned his too-knowing gaze on Vinny. "I know. I came in to check on you."

"You did?" Vinny furrowed his brow. "I don't remember that."

He remembered the pain, and then a voice leading him away from the darkness, telling him he was safe.

"What was the nightmare about?"

"The usual." Vinny tried to shrug it off. "Being beaten by Hunter."

"I still dream about that," Lyle admitted. "Either that or wandering through the forest alone."

Vinny shivered, knowing he'd been lucky. He'd not disappeared as Lyle had. If Gruff hadn't found Lyle, half-dead in the snow, Vinny would never have been rescued and it would have been his turn to disappear next week. Vinny would never have been chosen by the green coats to be a companion. He wasn't sweet and pliable as they liked them.

Maybe that's what Damien wanted. A sweet twink to warm his bed.

He hugged his knees to his chest. "Do you think Damien doesn't like me because I'm not sweet and gentle like you." It mortified him to ask but he had to know the truth. "I could be sweet and gentle."

It would kill him, but he'd try if he had to.

Lyle squeezed his arm. "No, Vinny. Remember what I said. Damien wants you. Not some faceless twink."

"He tells me he won't let me go. He cuddles me in bed and holds me close." Vinny grimaced. "But he's never here when I wake up."

"He let you sleep in," Lyle pointed out. "He threatened everyone with bodily harm if they woke you up."

"*You* woke me up," Vinny said sourly.

"There's nothing he can do to me." Lyle's smirk was smug. "Gruff would have him by the throat." Then Lyle blinked. "Are you growling?"

"He'd better not lay a finger on my Daddy," Vinny said, his tone fierce.

Lyle's lips twitched. "Your Daddy, huh?"

"Mine." Vinny was sure of that.

"You're gonna quit whining now?"

Before Vinny could snap back, the door opened again and Damien came in, frowning when he saw Lyle sitting close to Vinny.

Lyle must have understood the reason for the glower because he stood, smiling down at Vinny. "Breakfast will be ready in fifteen minutes. Don't be late."

He slipped past Damien with a murmured "Don't upset him."

Damien frowned. "What did he mean by that?"

Vinny held out his hand. "Nothing. He was just worried about the dream." He tugged Damien down to sit next to him. When Damien left a gap between them, Vinny snuggled closer. He was done being subtle. "I missed you when I woke up."

Damien looked down at their joined hands as if he wasn't sure what just happened, but he didn't make any attempt to pull away. That was good, because Vinny wasn't going to let go of him ever.

"I had to ride up top."

"On that big horse?" Vinny was not a fan of horses and Damien's stallion was twice the size of the others in the stables.

Damien's lips twitched. "Thunder is a sweetheart."

"I'm a sweetheart," Vinny muttered. "Thunder is just scary."

"I'll take you out for a ride on him so you can make friends."

Vinny would rather peel potatoes for the next year than sit on Thunder's back. But he'd do it for Damien. He'd do anything that would bring him closer to this big, gruff Daddy bear.

"You won't let him run away with me?" he begged.

"I'll sit behind you," Damien promised.

Vinny sighed and leaned against Damien, snuggling as close as he could get. "You hold me tight, and I'll be fine."

"Vinny."

Vinny heard the note in Damien's voice change and knowing Damien was about to pull away, he reached up, slid his hand around Damien's neck and tugged him down to kiss him.

Their lips almost touching, Damien froze.

"Please, Daddy," Vinny begged. "Please."

He didn't know what he was begging for, only that he didn't want Damien to pull away now.

Then Damien groaned and hauled Vinny into his lap. Vinny locked his arms around Damien's neck and kissed him. He finally had his Daddy in his arms, and he was never letting him go.

Chapter 4

Damien

Vinny's slender arms were locked tightly around Damien's neck. His lips on Damien's seemed to loosen the knot of tension Damien didn't know he had inside him. All the men Damien had kissed before, all the boys who'd offered their submission to him, they were forgotten in the thrilled of feeling Vinny's mouth. Inexperienced and untrained, but somehow just right for him.

Damien never wanted to let Vinny go. He would be the one to train Vinny, to show him what it was like to love and be loved. He had his naked boy in his arms. Vinny was hard already, and Damien felt his own cock stiffen under the flexing of Vinny's thigh muscles.

He tugged Vinny closer to him, deepening the kiss, coaxing Vinny's mouth open wider to slide his tongue against Vinny's, to lead them in a dance together.

He ran his hand over the scarred skin of Vinny's back down to cup his ass. He ignored the flames in his head as he thought about how Vinny had acquired those scars and focused on his boy.

Then he pressed a tender kiss against Vinny's smooth cheek. The boy barely had to shave at all.

"I love you, Daddy."

It was as if someone threw ice water over Damien.

He broke free of Vinny's embrace, lifted the boy onto the bed and threw himself back, out of Vinny's reach.

"What's wrong, Daddy?"

Damien had to ignore Vinny's hurt voice. "I can't do this, Vinny. It isn't right. You're too young."

He saw the hurt in Vinny's eyes, then the fury gather in his expression.

"I'm the same age as Lyle," Vinny snapped, breathing hard Damien suspected so he wouldn't break down in tears. He seemed so much younger than Lyle although only a handful of weeks separated them. "I'm going to be eighteen next week."

"And I'm forty. I'm old enough to be your father."

"How many times do we have to have this conversation? I don't want a father, I want you. No one else."

Damien shook his head. "I can't do this, Vinny. What you want and what you need are not the same thing. It's my job to make sure you get what you need."

"And you think you know what that is?" Vinny scrambled off the bed and threw on an old T-shirt and sweats. "You're wrong. But don't you worry. I'll find myself someone who wants to be my

Daddy. Someone younger and handsome."

The last three words pricked Damien's heart, but he tried to keep his expression blank. "Maybe that would be for the best."

Vinny stared at him. "How can you be so stupid?" He stormed out of the bedroom and down the stairs.

Damien sighed, knowing he'd hurt his boy again. Why did trying to do the right thing always left them both feeling like crap? He had to make it right, even if he couldn't get Vinny to understand why he wouldn't make love to him. He followed Vinny into the kitchen and of course all the brothers had to be there, the kitchen table littered with empty plates and cups.

Lyle's expression changed when he saw Vinny's expression. "What's wrong?" He turned on Damien who took a step back. "I told you not to upset him."

He got up to comfort Vinny, but PJ was there first. Before Damien could stop him, Vinny was in PJ's embrace.

"Don't you worry, Vinny. I'll take care of you if big brother won't." PJ bent his head as if he were going to kiss him.

Flames exploded inside Damien's head. "No!" he roared, yanking Vinny out of PJ's arms.

"Well, if you don't want him," PJ joked.

Before Damien's brain kicked in, he'd swung a right hook into PJ's cheek. Despite his size, PJ wasn't prepared for the sudden force of the blow. He staggered back, only prevented from ending up on the floor by Jake and Alec taking each arm and holding him upright.

Everyone was frozen in place. There was silence in the kitchen. The only sound Damien could hear was the blood pumping in his head. He could see the shock on his brother's faces. Damien had never hit any of his siblings. He'd always been the calm one, the one to break up their fights. Damien watched as blood dripped out of PJ's nose and hit the floor.

At that moment the world started again.

"What the hell, Damien?" Vinny's voice cracked.

"What the hell did you do that for?" Jake yelled, glaring at Damien.

Damien chose Vinny to focus his attention on, not sure he wouldn't hit his brother again. "You were in his arms. He was about to kiss you."

Vinny's mouth twisted bitterly. "At least he wants me. Unlike you."

"That's not true," Damien protested. "I'm trying to do the right thing here."

Vinny's green eyes blazed at him. "By rejecting me? By hitting PJ? That's some twisted up sense of right you've got there. You could be a green coat."

He turned on his heel and stalked out of the kitchen.

Silence again, then Lyle turned on Damien.

"You idiot!"

Damien took a step back as Lyle shouted at him. Lyle's cheeks were crimson, and he clenched his fists. Damien wasn't sure if Lyle was about to launch at him. He frowned at Lyle and saw Gruff glower at him as he moved next to his boy.

"He's a minor. No one should be kissing him," Damien snapped, ignoring the fact that five minutes ago he'd been doing just that.

"I don't care about that," Lyle yelled. "Do you have any clue what Vinny's life was like? How much he was abused and beaten in the tower? He was the kid all the green coats picked on. The one they used as an example to cower the others. No one wanted to end up like Vinny."

Damien knew. He'd sat through night after night of Vinny screaming and begging not to be hurt again. Vinny's nightmares about being in the tower made Damien break out in a cold sweat. But hearing it out loud made him flinch. From the outside the tower looked like a fairy tale. But what lay inside had made burly law enforcement want to vomit when they rescued the kids. Damien was pleased he'd never been allowed inside.

"You brought him here and promised you'd take care of him," Lyle said in a quieter voice.

"I am," Damien protested.

"By thumping your brother. Do you think violence is the way to take care of an abused kid like Vinny?"

Lyle didn't wait for an answer. He left the kitchen and Damien heard him thumping up the stairs.

"Way to go, Damien," Harry said, and Damien had never heard that icy tone aimed at him before.

Damien walked out before he lost it again. He was angry, but now at himself, not his brothers. He had no idea how to make this right.

Vinny's bedroom door was closed and when Damien stopped to listen, his heart wrenched at the distraught sound of Vinny weeping. Damien heard Lyle soothing him, knowing it should be him in there. Then he heard his name mentioned. Damien gave a wry smile at Vinny's response. That was a five-dollar donation to the jar.

He raised his hand to knock, then lowered his arm and went into his bedroom. Damien swiftly packed a small backpack. He'd find a motel for a couple of days and give everyone space before he did something stupid—more stupid. Damien picked up the pack and hurried out of his bedroom before he changed his mind. It was all quiet in Vinny's room now.

Gruff was at the bottom of the stairs, holding a cup of coffee. He eyed Damien's pack. "Running away won't help, Damien."

"I'm not running away." Damien said, ignoring the lizard thought in his head pointing out that's exactly what he was about to do.

Gruff raised an eyebrow. "Oh?"

"I just need to calm down."

"You're an idiot," Gruff informed him. "So is PJ but he always is."

"Thanks for that," PJ yelled but they both ignored him.

"I'm not the right person for Vinny. He needs a parental figure now."

Gruff rolled his eyes. "You know exactly what Vinny needs and it ain't a parent. Go upstairs and tell him you're sorry."

Damien hesitated. He wanted nothing more

than to run up the stairs, gather Vinny into his arms, take him into Damien's large bedroom, and show him how much he was loved. But Vinny was seventeen. And Damien couldn't go around thumping people who kissed Vinny. That way lay madness. One day he would watch a handsome Daddy take Vinny from him. Damien's fate had been laid out thirty years or more ago. He knew that. He just needed space to get his head sorted.

"Take care of him," he muttered.

"You're an idiot," Gruff said.

"So you keep saying but I'm the one responsible for him." It wasn't strictly true. As Vinny was so close to majority, the authorities had chosen to focus on the younger boys and left Vinny in Lyle's charge. But the Brenners had all known it was merely a formality. Vinny had always been Damien's. "It's what I've got to do."

Damien hurried out of the cabin before he made a bigger fool of himself, and headed for his truck, not looking back.

Vinny

Vinny spent most of the day hiding in his bedroom, distraught. He knew the whole thing was his fault, no matter what Lyle said. He was the one who'd kissed Damien. If he'd just waited for his birthday, his Daddy wouldn't have had to feel so noble and reject him.

Lyle tried to comfort Vinny. "Damien is just being an idiot."

"My Daddy is not an idiot," Vinny snapped.

Lyle's lips twitched, but he said, "I'm sorry. I shouldn't have been rude about your Daddy."

"Even if he is being an idiot." Vinny huffed.

"Don't give up on Damien," Lyle urged him. "It's clear Damien cares for you deeply."

Vinny gave him a dubious look. "Are you sure?"

Lyle smiled at him fondly. "I'm sure and so is Gruff. I know what the brothers are like, and Damien especially has this fixed idea of what is right and wrong. He's only trying to do the right thing for you."

"Even if it's not what I want?"

"*Especially* if it's not what you want," Lyle said with a rueful smile.

They both looked up at the knock at the door.

Vinny hoped against hope that was Damien, but PJ poked his head around the door. Vinny sagged but PJ looked miserable with the darkening bruise on his cheekbone.

"Are you all right," Vinny asked, patting the space next to him.

"I should ask you that." PJ came in and sat gingerly on the bed. He was so large he seemed to swallow up the air in the room, but Vinny knew better than to tease PJ about it. The man was very sensitive about his size.

Vinny glanced at Lyle as PJ seemed to take an age to start talking, then his words tumbled out of his mouth in a rush.

"I've come to apologize, Vinny. I'm so sorry. I tease Damien all the time, but I never meant to get between you two. I know how you feel about each other."

He paused, seeming to expect an answer, and Vinny nodded. Damien was always at the mercy of PJ's teasing, but to be fair, PJ did it to everyone.

"This is the first time Damien's ever cared enough to be possessive," PJ said, touching the bruise with a wince. "It's the first time he's ever hit any of us. The man can pack a punch." He sounded almost impressed. "But honestly, Vinny, don't give up on Damien."

Vinny almost laughed in PJ's face. He should be grateful PJ tried to make him feel better, but Vinny wished people wouldn't keep telling him not to give up on Damien. It was clear Damien had given up on him.

"Let's go downstairs," Lyle suggested. "You need to eat something, Vinny."

Vinny was sure he was going to barf if he put anything in his mouth, but Lyle insisted, and PJ looked relieved that he could stop talking about feelings.

They were having a subdued lunch when there was a knock on the door. Not Damien then. He wouldn't knock. Vinny gave up the pretense of eating and quit pushing the food around the plate.

Alec opened the door and grinned at the young guy with sleek, light brown hair and soft brown eyes. "Hi, Matt," Alec said with obvious surprise. "I wasn't expecting you today."

"I have intel on one of our cases."

"Come into the office. Jake?"

"On my way," Jake said and stuffed food into his mouth.

Matt received a chorus of hi's from the

brothers. They all seemed to know him. He waved at them all as he walked through to the office.

Vinny glanced at Lyle who gave a slight nod. They knew who Matt was to Alec, a sometime boy, but they weren't sure if Alec knew who Matt really was. Alec was always closed-mouthed about Matt.

When everyone had disappeared from the kitchen and Vinny and Lyle were left to clear up, Vinny voiced his concerns.

"When is Matt going to tell Alec the truth?"

Lyle twisted the dishcloth in his hands. "Maybe he doesn't want Alec to know. If he says who he is, he's got to get involved and you know Matt doesn't want to be dragged into it."

No one had been more surprised than Lyle and Vinny when they'd discovered the boy who'd refused to settle down with Alec, but somehow kept coming back to him, was George, the boy who was great with horses. They'd believed George had been disappeared on his eighteenth birthday, but here he was, several years later, with a different name and a secret past.

"We really need to get Matt alone," Vinny muttered.

"You think Matt wants that? He's been avoiding us since we got here." Lyle sounded resigned and Vinny sighed in agreement.

Matt did not want to talk to his former friends, which Vinny thought was sad. He wanted to keep his connections with the past, however painful they were. The boys in the theme park had been the closest to family he had. But he knew not everyone thought like him. Maybe Matt would change his mind. Vinny and Lyle would be here if he did.

Despite his best efforts and those of the brothers to cheer him up, Vinny had had more than enough by the time the evening arrived. Lyle helped him clean up after dinner and offered to sit with him, but he cried off pleading a headache and went to bed early.

He didn't sleep, spending most of the night staring miserably at the ceiling. When he did sleep his dreams were full of nightmares and pain, but this time there was no one to comfort him. By four in the morning, he'd had enough. Vinny crawled out of bed and went downstairs to make breakfast.

He was busy stirring oatmeal when he heard a truck rumbling down the drive. He looked out of the window, but it was too dark to see outside.

Damien!

Vinny didn't dare hope but who else would it be? All the bedroom doors had been closed except Damien's.

He kept stirring the oatmeal, but also quickly hunted out steak and eggs. Damien only ate oatmeal under protest.

It seemed to take an age before he heard footsteps on the stoop, but he would know that heavy tread from anywhere.

Damien had come home.

Chapter 5

Damien

Damien spent a miserable evening in a gay bar he knew well, drinking beer after beer and staring down into his glass. Boys approached him. Sweet twinks with hopeful smiles on their faces. But he turned them all away. The only boy he wanted was probably hating on him right now. He signaled the bartender for another beer, but the man shook his head.

"You're done, Damien."

Damien's jaw dropped open. "You're cutting me off already, Aaron?"

The bartender, a huge bear of a man almost as big as PJ and just as bushy a beard, gave him a sympathetic look. "Go home. Sort whatever's going on with your boy."

But he wasn't drunk or causing a fight. He was just...drinking. And sulking. Yeah, he was doing a lot of sulking.

"You're making the place miserable, and all the boys are huddled together trying to work out how to make you happy. This is making the other guys unhappy. Get out of here before some idiot decides to start a fight."

Damien looked up and realized Aaron was right. The boys were huddled in one corner shooting him worried glances and the other guys were sending him angry looks. He needed to get out of there before someone decided to challenge him. In the mood he was in he could easily end up spending the night behind bars.

He stumbled back to the cheap motel, unsteady on his feet. Maybe he'd had more to drink than he thought. As Damien stripped off his clothes, he caught sight of his face in the mirror. Aaron had been right again. He looked wrecked. He looked *old*.

Damien lay awake all night. The bed was adequate, but it didn't take a genius to realize he was stupid sleeping in a motel when he could be at home in his own bed. He had no friends he could go to for a shoulder to cry on. His brothers were his friends and family. And they all thought he was an idiot. An ugly idiot duckling.

Finally, about four o'clock in the morning, Damien gave up trying to sleep, got dressed, and drove home to face the music.

Damien drove slowly up the mountain road to the cabin, cursing under his breath when he saw lights in the kitchen. He'd hoped he'd be able to sneak in before anyone was awake. He was tempted to drive away again but he told himself to man up and behave like a goddamn Daddy.

He cut the engine and took a deep breath. What did Gruff say? Was he a Daddy or a mouse? He got out of the car and straightened his shoulders. He was a Daddy. He could do this. He could do the right thing for Vinny.

Damien walked into the kitchen to find Vinny making breakfast and all his resolutions fled in the face of Vinny's tear-filled red eyes and blotchy face. Vinny had obviously had no more sleep than Damien had.

"Sit down," Vinny said dully. "Breakfast is almost ready."

Damien hoped and prayed one of his brothers would join them, but from the silence in the rest of the cabin it looked as if he was out of luck. Damien sat in his usual seat. He could tell Vinny wanted to ignore him by the way he refused to look at him. But it wasn't in the boy to ignore his Daddy. Vinny handed him his breakfast. Damien counted himself lucky he wasn't wearing the eggs and steak.

Vinny covered the rest of the food and sat opposite him, nursing a glass of milk.

"You're not eating?" Damien asked. Each mouthful was probably as delicious as usual but tasted like ashes in his mouth.

"I'm not hungry."

The dull, unhappy voice was killing Damien. He wanted to drag Vinny into his lap and rock him until Vinny smiled again.

"I need to know the answer to something," Vinny said.

Damien looked at him warily, sensing he wasn't going to like the question. "Okay."

Vinny took a deep breath. "I'm gonna ask a question and if the answer is yes, I'll be out of the cabin by the end of the day, and I won't bother you again."

Damien waited, worried about what he'd ask.

Vinny looked at him then, his green eyes clouded. "Did you sleep with anyone last night?"

Damien hesitated, taken aback by the question.

Vinny seemed to shrink into himself. "I'll go pack. I'd like to say goodbye to Lyle if you don't mind."

As he stood, Damien suddenly realized what was about to happen. "No, Vinny, wait."

He rushed around the table before Vinny could leave. Damien eased him back down in the chair. Vinny seemed ready to bolt so Damien knelt in front of Vinny and took his hands. He wasn't going to let Vinny go anywhere. "Vinny, I would never cheat on you. I'm not made that way."

The boy didn't look convinced, but he didn't tug his hands away.

"I went to a gay bar last night, but I never slept with anyone. I got offers from sweet twinks. I won't deny that. But I said no to all of them. My heart is and always will be only for you...and the bartender cut me off," Damien added the last part ruefully.

Vinny smiled but he was obviously still worried. Damien pressed a kiss to Vinny's palm. He didn't know how else to convince his boy. Then he placed Vinny's hand over his heart.

"I love you, Vinny. My heart is yours."

And of course that was the moment one of his brothers chose to walk into the kitchen.

Gruff grinned at the sight of Damien on his knees. "Hey guys. Come in here. Big brother is on his knees."

"It ain't the first time," Harry said.

Damien groaned as Vinny's face darkened.

The brothers crowded in to stare at them like he and Vinny were some kind of circus act.

"Shut up. Just shut up," Damien begged. "I'm trying to apologize to my boy. You're not helping."

"'Bout time you pulled your head out of your ass," Brad said, walking past them to investigate what was under the covered plates. "Is this for us?"

Damien sighed and focused on Vinny again. "I think the moment is lost. Will you forgive me for walking out on you?"

Vinny nodded tightly.

"And you won't leave me?"

Another nod.

Damien leaned forward and kissed Vinny gently on his mouth. "I'll take you to bed after this. I can see you need sleep."

He looked up to see PJ hanging awkwardly by the kitchen door, a big bruise darkening one cheek. Damien stood and held out his arms. The relief on his brother's face was instantaneous. Damien realized how much his brothers still relied on their big brother. Him having a meltdown wasn't helping anyone.

PJ grabbed Damien into a bear hug which nearly squeezed the life out of him. "I'm so sorry for being an ass, Damien. I won't ever do that again."

"You'd better not," Damien growled, but then he lightly touched PJ's cheek. "I'm so sorry for hitting you."

"You pack a mean punch, brother," PJ said. "But I deserved it."

"Have we all kissed and made up now?" Jake said, but Damien could see the worry in his eyes. Jake hated confrontation of any sort, particularly between his brothers.

"We're fine," Damien agreed.

There was a moment when all the brothers swirled around him, making sure they hugged him and each other. The ugly duckling was welcomed back into the fold once more. When they stepped back, he took a breath and forced a smile.

"Eat breakfast before it gets cold," he suggested.

Each brother sought his gaze one by one and reassured, headed for the stovetop.

Damien looked for Vinny, but he was gone. Panicked, Damien took a step toward the door when Lyle stopped him with a gentle hand on his arm.

"I sent him upstairs. He's exhausted."

Damien gave a curt nod and bounded up the stairs. Vinny's door was ajar. Damien breathed a sigh of relief. He'd made it a rule that no one was allowed in when the door was closed unless Vinny agreed. Vinny had so little to control in his life, Damien could at least give him his bedroom. If he knocked and Vinny said no that rule would apply to him too. But the door was open, which meant he could walk in.

Vinny was on the bed, still fully dressed, his back to the door. Damien sat down on the bed and ran a hand down Vinny's back.

Vinny expelled a long breath. "Lie down with me?"

Damien spooned around Vinny and tucked the boy into his larger frame. "You need to sleep."

"So do you."

"Then we'll rest for the morning. You don't move from my arms unless you need a leak, and then you ask."

"Is that an order?" Vinny asked.

"Yes." It was definitely an order.

"Okay then." Vinny sounded happy with that. He pressed a kiss against Damien's arm. "I can live with that."

Vinny

The day of Vinny's eighteenth birthday arrived. He awoke in his little room feeling a weight off his shoulders. He couldn't be disappeared now. Even though the risk had been small, it had kept him awake at night. But now he was eighteen. No one from Kingdom Mountain or any of the other theme parks would be interested in him again. He was too old for them.

There was one thing missing however. Where was Damien?

He had expectations. He thought he'd be woken up with a mouth around his cock or an invitation to make his Daddy a very happy bear. But there was nothing except the sound of his alarm to get up and help Lyle with breakfast.

Vinny pressed his lips together. "You promised,

Daddy. You promised!"

Damien had promised him things would be different from today. But there was no sound at all from the next room and when he opened his bedroom door, he found Damien's door wide open. His Daddy had gotten up without even giving Vinny a morning kiss.

That hurt. Didn't his Daddy want to love him on his special day?

He shut the door and sat on his bed, unsure what to do. Should he wait for Damien?

His bedroom door opened, and Vinny looked up with a smile. It faded fast when he saw Lyle.

"Oh good, you're awake," Lyle said. "Hurry up. We've got to fix breakfast early as we've got to clean the cabin."

Vinny stared at him. "Today?"

Lyle wrinkled his brow. "Yes. Why?"

"You want me to clean the cabin today."

"Yes, all of the guys are out this morning. Damien said something about a special delivery. They'll be back just after lunch. I'll see you downstairs."

Lyle vanished and clattered down the stairs, leaving Vinny fuming and glaring at the door.

"Happy fucking birthday, Vinny. Welcome to being an adult."

And no, he wasn't going to pay the damned dollar...two dollars.

Vinny didn't stop working from the time he got up until lunchtime. By now he was familiar with the routine of the cabin, but Lyle kept finding jobs for him. Sweep the grates, clean the bathrooms, change the bedlinens.

Vinny sniffled miserably as he scrubbed the big tub in Damien's bedroom. It was no different than any other birthday at Kingdom Mountain. Why he thought his eighteenth should be any different he didn't know. But he had. Vinny had expected to spend his birthday in his Daddy's arms, sit on his Daddy's lap, and feel his Daddy push his thick cock inside him for the first time. He sniffled again and tears slid down his nose to fall in the tub. He scrubbed them away furiously.

"Vinny. You've got the potatoes to do!" Lyle yelled.

Vinny sat back on his haunches. Who died and made Lyle the king of the vegetable peeler? It was his birthday, dammit. Okay, Lyle nearly died on his own birthday, so maybe Vinny couldn't complain too much. But Lyle wasn't the boss of him. Where was Damien? He was Vinny's boss. But Lyle wouldn't tell him. Lyle wouldn't tell him anything except give him more orders.

Would Damien get him a gift? Vinny had never had a present before. He hoped Damien didn't give him a horse. Lyle may love the horses, Vinny not so much.

"Vinny! Potatoes!"

Vinny stomped down the stairs and glowered at Lyle.

"Finally!" Lyle said impatiently as he stirred something in a pan on the stovetop. "I thought you'd drowned in there. Peel the potatoes."

Vinny looked at the mound which covered half

the table. He was going to be there forever. He sat at the table and picked up the first potato. A tear dripped onto the skin. Vinny sniffled, but Lyle ignored him as he cooked.

Just before lunchtime all the brothers trooped into the kitchen, except Damien.

"Oh, thank God," Lyle snapped. "Where the hell have you been?"

"We got held up," Gruff said, walking over to give Lyle a tender kiss which made Lyle melt into his arms and Vinny grit his teeth.

"I was running out of chores," Lyle said somewhat breathlessly.

Vinny hadn't noticed any lack of things for him to do.

"You can stand down now," Damien assured him as he walked into the kitchen, carrying a box with a ribbon loosely tied around it.

Even though Vinny was angry with Damien, his heart still skipped a beat at the sight of him. He was so focused on Damien he almost missed what Lyle said.

"You better not have made me lose my best friend," Lyle said. "I'm not the right man to give orders."

"You didn't have any problem barking out the orders today," Vinny said, his lip wobbling.

Damien enfolded Vinny in his arms. "That was my fault, baby boy. I asked Lyle to keep you busy. I didn't expect to be so long."

Vinny tilted his head to look up at him. "But why?"

"I have a present for you. I had to get it today.

Come and look." Damien pushed the box toward him. "Happy birthday, Vinny."

Vinny stared at it but didn't make any move to open it. "This is for me?"

"It's for you." When Vinny didn't make a move, Damien asked, "Aren't you going to open it?"

"It's not a horse, is it?"

Damien's lips twitched. "No, it's not a horse, I promise." He pushed the box toward Vinny. "I think you should open it."

All the misery of the morning suddenly vanished. This was Vinny's first ever present. He stared at Damien who nodded, then he tugged on the ribbon and opened the box. His mouth fell open as he spied the sleepy contents.

"Daddy!"

It was a tiny black puppy with white paws and a heart-shaped white patch on its chest. The pup opened one eye at him and yawned.

"You got me a puppy?"

Damien nodded. "He's an orphan. He's twelve weeks old. His momma passed away and his owners reared the litter by hand. This little guy is the last one to be chosen. He needs a good home."

"He's an orphan just like me," Vinny said, stroking the pup's soft, silky fur on his head. "What is he?"

"He's a real mixture. But his momma was medium size and she loved running in the trees and sleeping in front of the stove. I think this little guy will fit in well here."

"Can I hold him?"

"Of course you can. He's tired at the moment

because we took him for a potty break."

"The reason we're late is we couldn't catch him," Harry muttered. "He's one lively dog."

Vinny gently scooped him into his arms. The puppy yawned and grumbled, then settled down to sleep. "What's his name?"

Damien smiled at him. "You can name him. He's your dog."

"Really?" Vinny had never had anything of his own before, let alone been responsible for it. "I think he looks like a Rexy."

"Rexy. That's a good name." Damien put his arm around Vinny and gently stroked the puppy.

"Can we give him the rest of the presents now?" Gruff demanded. "And eat? I'm starving."

Vinny stared at Gruff wide-eyed. "More presents? For me?"

PJ staggered in with a dog basket piled high with wrapped boxes. "Happy birthday, little brother."

The breath caught in Vinny's throat. He was one of the family now. He blinked back the tears. That was the biggest present he could imagine. Then he glanced up at Damien who was studying him closely. Almost the biggest present.

Lyle came over with a small gift. "Forgive me for making you peel potatoes on your birthday?"

Vinny eyed the gift suspiciously. "This isn't a vegetable peeler, is it?"

Lyle chuckled. "No. You're safe."

"Do I have to keep doing the potatoes now I'm family?" Vinny demanded. "Because that job sucks."

"We'll rotate the job," Damien promised. He held up his hand as PJ opened his mouth. "Including you."

PJ huffed but subsided without another word.

Vinny opened Lyle's present to discover it was a cell phone. He'd never had a phone of his own.

"From Gruff and me," Lyle said.

"Thank you. Thanks so much." Vinny flung his arms around Lyle's neck, then hugged Gruff.

"You're welcome, little brother," Gruff said.

"Open the others," Damien urged.

Vinny turned to the pile in the dog bed. For someone who'd never received a single gift it was almost overwhelming. There were brand new clothes, just for him, from PJ. And a collar and leash for Rexy from Harry, plus a pile of treats and toys. Brad brought him a chemistry set and told him he'd help him blow stuff up. But the gift that made Vinny burst into tears was in a plain white envelope.

Jake handed it to him, almost nervously. "This is from me and Alec."

Vinny opened the slim envelope to discover a single sheet of paper. Confused, he looked at Jake.

"Take it out," Jake urged.

Vinny did, and stared at the form, not sure what he was looking at.

"It's a birth certificate," Damien told him.

Vincent read the name out loud, sounding out the syllables as Gruff had taught him. "Vin...cent Col...man." Vinny's hands shook as he looked at Jake. "This is me?"

"It is. Look, it confirms today really is your

eighteenth birthday." Jake hesitated, then he said, "Your mom died giving birth to you and your dad couldn't cope. He gave you up for adoption. He probably had no idea what would happen to you."

"Is my dad still alive?" Vinny asked, not sure if he wanted to know the answer.

"We're trying to track him down," Alec said.

"Thank you." Vinny's voice wobbled. "I—I have a name now."

Then he turned to bury his face in Damien's chest, sobbing because for the first time in his life he had a name that was his, and a family he'd lost.

Chapter 6

Damien

Damien rocked his boy as he sobbed, crooning incoherent words of love in his ear. He wanted Vinny to know he was safe and wanted and loved. His dad may have abandoned him, but he had a new family and a lover and a Daddy now.

The brothers tactfully left them alone for a while to give Vinny a chance to recover. Finally, the tears dried enough for Vinny to calm. He stroked Rexy who whimpered, seeming to sense his new owner was upset and needed comfort.

"I never cried when I was at Kingdom Mountain. Now all I seem to do is cry," Vinny said ruefully.

"Your life was stable at Kingdom Mountain. It was a horrible life, but stable, and all you've ever known. Now your world has turned upside down, including finding out who you are."

"I really am Vinny." Vinny sounded bemused. "I thought it was just a name they assigned me."

"Would you prefer we called you Vincent or something else?" Damien asked.

Vinny thought about it for a while, then shook his head. "I'm Vinny and always will be. I made myself Vinny." He leaned back against Damien with a contented sigh.

"Happy?" Damien murmured and pressed a kiss into his hair.

"So happy."

"Your birthday isn't over yet," Damien said, and Vinny fidgeted at the heated promise in Damien's voice.

"You can fuck him later, Damien. It's the birthday boy's dinner first." PJ already had the dollar out to go into the jar.

Damien was tempted to pick Vinny up and take him upstairs just because he could, and he wanted to be buried inside his boy. But the birthday dinner was a tradition, although he wasn't letting Vinny off his lap.

Vinny looked at the plate of chicken pot pie in front of him and then at Lyle. "You made this for me?"

"It's your favorite meal." Lyle smiled at him. "And you deserve it for peeling all those potatoes."

Vinny's lip wobbled again. "Did you get this for your birthday?"

Lyle grinned at him. "I got to wake up naked on top of a furry bear instead of dying. And it got busy after I was rescued."

"Vinny has a point," Harry said. "You didn't get to celebrate. We'll arrange that soon."

"And I get to be king of the vegetable peeler," Vinny declared.

Harry blinked at him. "If you say so."

"Did you see how many potatoes he made me peel?"

"Blame your Daddy's late arrival," Lyle said. "I was desperate. I had no idea how else to keep you occupied."

"Can I blame the puppy?" Damien asked.

"No," Lyle snapped.

"No way." Vinny clutched Rexy to him. "You can't blame the puppy. He doesn't know what he's supposed to be doing."

Damien sighed.

"Eat your pie," Lyle said.

Vinny went to pick up the fork, but Damien took it from him.

"I'm going to feed my boy."

Vinny flushed but he nodded.

"No dogs at the table," Lyle said firmly.

Damien thought Vinny might argue from the way he clutched onto Rexy, but he slipped off Damien's lap and laid Rexy in his bed, tucking a soft blanket covered with bears around him.

"The Daddy Bears love you, Rexy," Vinny murmured.

This boy made Damien's heart skip a beat. The puppy whimpered, then went back to sleep. Vinny returned to sit on Damien's lap and waited for him to dip into the pie. Damien could feel the tension in Vinny at the idea of being fed.

Vinny hadn't seen the boys come and go over the years. All different, some littles, some older. All welcome at the table because that's the way the Brenners were. But when Vinny realized no one seemed bothered by him being fed and he kind of liked it, he relaxed to Damien's relief, and enjoyed his birthday treat.

By the time the pot pie was finished, Vinny was sleepy and burrowed into Damien for a nap.

"Don't fall asleep yet, my boy," Damien said, knowing what was coming next.

Vinny blinked sleepily at him. "Can we go upstairs to sleep?"

Damien planned to go upstairs but sleeping definitely wasn't on his mind. "Soon, my boy. One thing first." He nodded at Lyle.

Vinny sat up, the pouty expression changing when Harry came in with a large cake with candles. The cake was in the shape of a puppy who looked remarkably like Rexy with the white paws and patch on its chest.

Damien joined in the Happy Birthday chorus, led by Jake, and Rexy raised his head and joined in with puppy yips. Damien wasn't surprised to see Vinny's eyes brimming with tears again. He doubted Vinny was going to forget this day for the rest of his life. "Happy birthday, my boy."

"It's chocolate cake," Harry told him. "Lyle said you were never allowed chocolate cake at the theme park."

Vinny shook his head, still too teary to speak.

"Blow your candles out, Vinny," Brad said.

Vinny leaned forward and blew all the candles out in one go and everyone clapped.

"First slice to the birthday boy," Lyle said, armed with a knife to cut the cake.

But Vinny shook his head again. "First slice goes to you, Lyle. Without you, I'd never have gotten here and found my Daddy."

Lyle smiled at him. "We'll share it."

Damien wanted to hug them both. He would have done if he hadn't been sure Gruff would have killed him for laying a hand on Lyle. The Brenner bears were very possessive about their boys. He caught Gruff giving him the side-eye and he rolled his eyes.

Gruff huffed and then grinned at him. "Was it that obvious?"

Lyle nudged him gently. "For brothers that are as tactile and huggy as you guys, you're a nightmare when it comes to us."

"Just the way it should be," Alec said.

Everyone looked at him in surprise. Unless they were talking business, Alec was the quietest of the brothers.

He noticed them all staring at him. "What?"

Damien grinned at him. "We agree with you. It's just a surprise to hear you say it out loud."

Alec huffed and shrugged, and huffed again, and they laughed at him, because that's what the brothers did.

Damien waited until Vinny had finished his half slice of cake, then he stood, taking Vinny with him, grinning at his squeak. "I'm taking my boy upstairs and I don't want to be disturbed."

"Like we don't know what you're doing," Jake pointed out.

Vinny pressed his hot face into Damien's neck, but Damien didn't care who knew what he was about to do with his boy.

"You take care of Rexy for the afternoon," he ordered.

"We will," Lyle promised. "He's too young to

watch...whatever you're gonna do."

"Please stop," Vinny moaned.

Damien chuckled and carried Vinny up the stairs to his bedroom. He opened the door and paused to look at his boy. "You sleep in here from now, boy."

Vinny raised his head. "In your bed?"

"In *our* bed." Damien stressed the word because he wanted Vinny to be clear there was no negotiation. "Unless you're naughty. Then you might have to sleep in the small room as a punishment." He saw the horror on Vinny's face. Damien didn't give out punishments unless they were absolutely necessary, and then he adapted them to the individual boy. He had a feeling Vinny would not like being exiled from his Daddy.

But that was for another day. Today was all about loving and learning each other's bodies. He placed Vinny gently on the bed. "I've been waiting for this day forever," he murmured.

"You're not the only one," Vinny agreed, his arms still around Damien's neck. "This is it, Daddy? You're not going to run away from me again? It's you and me forever."

"You and me forever, boy," Damien agreed, realizing Vinny wasn't going to let him go anytime soon and if Damien wanted to keep his neck, then he'd better hug his boy until he was reassured. He picked Vinny up and sat with him on the bed, rocking him gently as he had when Vinny had cried. "There's nothing that would make me run from you again, Vinny. I love you."

"You don't think I'm too young for you?"

Trust his boy to put his finger right on Damien's sore spot.

"*I'm* too old for you," Damien said bluntly. "But you're the one that I love, and I hope you love me too."

He waited for Vinny's answer. The silence went on for a long time and eventually he tilted Vinny's chin to look into his limpid eyes.

"Boy?"

Vinny gave him a mischievous and heated smile. He placed a hand on Damien's cheek. "I love you, Daddy. And now I'd like you to fuck me through the mattress. You can pay the dollar later."

Damien pressed into Vinny's touch. "No dollar. Not this time. Just me fucking you."

Vinny

The growl Damien gave was very satisfying. His Daddy wanted him so much, and Vinny had waited patiently—for Vinny he'd been patient—like a good boy but now it was his turn. He placed Damien's large hand over his cock, already hard and so ready for his Daddy.

"Please?"

Then Damien moved suddenly, and Vinny found himself flat on his back and Damien leaning over him.

"Daddy," Vinny said breathlessly.

"Your Daddy," Damien said, and it sounded like a promise.

Vinny didn't know how Damien did it, but the clothes melted away from him and he was naked under Damien's larger, furry body, being pressed into the mattress, their leaking dicks sliding against each other. Vinny had dreamed of being held like this, knowing he couldn't go anywhere or do anything unless his Daddy allowed it. But unlike the fear he'd felt when the green coats tied him down, he felt nothing but excitement in Damien's arms.

Damien brushed his bushy beard over Vinny's skin. Vinny writhed underneath him as Damien took a slow tortuous path down his body, lips, tongue, and beard, driving him mad until Damien reached Vinny's cock.

Vinny melted as he felt a man's hot mouth around his cock for the first time. "So good," he moaned as Damien played and nibbled, feasting on his dick.

If Damien continued like this, there was no way Vinny was going to last until his Daddy was inside him, and he really wanted that.

"Please," he begged, tugging on Damien's thick hair. "Please."

Damien sucked hard and Vinny arched up, but then Damien pulled off and looked up at him, his lips and beard glistening.

"You're a tease," Vinny accused.

Damien's grin was positively devilish. "You have no idea."

He reached over Vinny to his drawer and pulled out condoms and lube.

Vinny bit his lip. He'd already told Damien he

didn't have to use condoms, but swiftly understood that Damien wouldn't do anything that could possibly harm him. Damien would go bare when he was tested and not before.

He gasped at the feel of the cool lube around his hole.

"I'll be gentle," Damien promised as he pressed one thick finger slowly inside him. At Vinny's hiss, Damien kissed him, his mouth demanding, distracting Vinny, until Vinny realized one finger had become two. Then Vinny shouted as Damien crooked his fingers and brushed something inside him.

"Good?" Damien murmured.

Vinny nodded frantically, his eyes so wide, clutching onto Damien for dear life. His focus narrowed down to the fingers in his ass. Two became three, but he needed more. He needed Damien's cock, and he begged Damien to fuck him.

"I can do that, my boy," Damien promised.

Vinny's channel clenched as Damien withdrew his fingers, and he had to fight not to spill hopelessly over his stomach. Soon Damien was back, kissing the tip of his cock to Vinny's hole.

"Breathe out," Damien ordered, then he pushed in so slowly until there was no space between them, buried root to tip.

"I can feel all of you." Vinny stared up at him open-mouthed, unable to breathe.

Just the sensation of Damien inside him was overwhelming at first. He was so full, it was too much. Tears squeezed out from the corner of his eyes. Damien seemed to understand and didn't move until Vinny managed a smile. Damien kissed the top of his nose and then his mouth, his kiss starting tender and then more forceful. He started short, shallow thrusts and Vinny clung onto Damien's strong biceps as Damien pushed him further up the bed, brushing Vinny's sweet spot until all Vinny could focus on was waiting for the next time stars would explode behind his eyes.

Vinny had been ready to come before they started and he tried to hold back his climax, but he came with a shout, his body shaking and clenching around his Daddy's, come spurting so hard it hit his chin. Somewhere in the aftershocks, he heard Damien roar above him and thrust hard into him before panting through his orgasm. Vinny couldn't speak, his muscles feeling like limp noodles, satiated, and happy.

Damien ignored the mess between them and wrapped his arms around Vinny who buried his face against Damien's chest.

"I'm never gonna let you go, my boy," Damien rumbled above him.

Vinny hung onto him with a ferocity Damien seemed to embrace. "I'll always be yours, Daddy." Emotion overcame him and he couldn't help the single tear that rolled down his cheek and into Damien's fur. How had he gotten so lucky?

Vinny rolled over and blinked sleepily at Damien who sat on the edge of the bed, rolling on a pair of socks. "Is it time to get up, Daddy?"

He must have slept all night. Well, not all night,

because his Daddy woke him up at least three times to remind himself what it was like to be buried inside Vinny's body. Which was why Vinny's ass ached so much. Vinny pressed down to feel that glorious ache.

"It is," Damien said, "but take your time. I'll make breakfast today. Get dressed when you're ready." Damien leaned over to give him a kiss. "And I want to see my boy in his new clothes."

"Yes, Daddy."

Damien grinned at him and left the bedroom, leaving Vinny staring up at the ceiling, a bit shell-shocked. Yesterday he'd woken in his little bedroom, an orphan boy who didn't even know if his name was his own. Today he was Vincent Colman, eighteen years old, and boy to the best Daddy in the world.

And judging by the squeaking outside the door, Daddy to a puppy who wanted attention. Vinny rolled out of bed and opened the door to find Rexy looking up at him.

"Hey, little guy. What are you doing up here all by yourself?" He picked Rexy up, who then enthusiastically licked his nose. Vinny giggled. "You sit on the bed and wait for me to shower."

He hoped Rexy didn't have an accident on the bed. He decided to take a quick shower just in case.

Once he'd returned to the bedroom, Rexy seemed relaxed, taking a quick puppy nap. Vinny smiled fondly at him. He couldn't quite believe the puppy was his. Then Vinny changed into new skinny jeans and long-sleeved T-shirt. He spent time admiring himself in the mirror. These were the first new clothes he'd ever owned. It was going to take time for him to recognize himself in the mirror. He noticed no one had bought him anything with green in it. If he could, Vinny would change his eye color in a heartbeat to the beautiful blue of his Daddy's.

Vinny tucked Rexy into his arms and left the bedroom. He hoped there was oatmeal left in the pan as he was feeling hungry now.

He was on the point of pushing the door open to the kitchen when he heard Damien mention his name and not in a "I love my boy," way he'd used all night.

"I'm sorry, Damien, but it's the only way to keep him safe."

Vinny waited to hear what his Daddy said as Jake sounded so grim.

"No, he stays here with me—us," Damien insisted. "I'm not letting my boy out of sight, and nobody is to tell him."

Vinny pressed his lips together. Tell him what? He hated the thought Damien was keeping secrets from him. He wasn't a little kid anymore.

"This is a green coat we're talking about. These are dangerous fuckers. You don't think when he turns up on the doorstep, Vinny might realize we've been keeping something from him?" Alec said.

"Dollar!" Harry said.

"Do we know the name of the man who escaped?" Brad asked over the sound of coins rattling.

"Flowers," Jake said.

"Yeah, Chase Flowers," Alec agreed.

Vinny felt the blood drain from his face. Of all the green coats Flowers frightened him the most. Flowers hated Vinny and would do anything he could to hurt him. He was a sadistic bastard who used to provoke Hunter into beating Vinny with the tawse. How had he escaped from custody? Vinny couldn't stay here. He had to get away before Flowers came after the Brenner family and tried to hurt them. The thought of Flowers hurting his Daddy made him feel sick.

"Let Jake and Alec take Vinny to a safe house," PJ suggested.

"No! Vinny's my boy and he stays with me," Damien exploded. "The only people I trust to take care of him are you guys, my brothers."

Jake huffed. Even without seeing him Vinny knew it was Jake. "Then Vinny gets an escort at all times. And Lyle. Someone needs to stay in the house with them."

"I have to use my laptop this morning," Brad said. "I can work down here with the little guys—sorry, Lyle. No offense."

"None taken," Lyle murmured. "But you need to talk to Vinny when he comes down. He isn't stupid."

"I will," Damien agreed.

Vinny ran as quietly as he could with Rexy to his bedroom. He couldn't take any chances with his family. Flowers would leave them alone when he realized Vinny was gone. He packed his clothes into an old backpack he found in the closet, hoping the brothers wouldn't mind him taking the hand-me-downs. Vinny left his new clothes behind, except for the ones he wore now. He couldn't take the time to change again. Damien would come looking for him soon.

"Take care of Daddy, Rexy." Vinny tickled Rexy under the chin. "I wish I could take you too, but I can't take the risk of the green coat hurting you and Daddy needs someone who loves him like we do."

He shut the door on Rexy's yipping, knowing the puppy would give him away. Damien would find him soon enough. Vinny jogged down the stairs and slipped out of the cabin, shutting the door oh-so-quietly. He prayed he wouldn't meet one of the brothers coming back in as he headed toward the mountain road and a scary, unknown future.

Chapter 7

Damien

The instant Damien realized Vinny had run away had been one of the worst moments of his life. Damien heard Rexy's frantic yelping and he'd walked into the little bedroom to find Vinny's few clothes gone from the closet along with an old backpack. He searched the whole of the top floor in case the boy was hiding but there was no sign of Vinny. How had he managed to slip out without anyone spotting him?

Damien pounded down the stairs, reaching for his jacket as fast as he could. His brothers crowded around him, all of them patting his back or squeezing his shoulder. It was comforting, if suffocating, but what he really wanted was his darling boy in his arms.

"Where's Vinny?" Gruff asked, his hand on Damien's shoulder.

"Gone," Damien said shortly.

"Gone where?" PJ looked confused.

"He's run away."

"No! He wouldn't do that," PJ exclaimed. "The boy is crazy about you."

"Look for yourself," Damien snapped. "He's

gone."

Just the thought of his boy alone on the mountain made Damien's heart twist. What if the green coats got him and he vanished forever?

"Keep it together, bro. We're on it. We'll get your boy back," Brad assured him.

There was a flurry of putting on coats and boots around him. Damien sat down on the bench, feeling defeated before he'd even started.

"I'll head for the top and work down," PJ announced, and he was out the door, along with Brad.

"We'll talk to our contacts," Jake said, and Alec nodded too. "Make sure the green coat isn't here yet." They vanished into the den, talking rapidly to each other.

"I'm taking Thunder," Damien said to Harry.

"I'll saddle him." Then Harry was gone, heading to the stables.

And then there was just Damien sitting on the bench, looking up at Gruff's and Lyle's worried expressions.

"Why did he leave me?" Damien asked, knowing he sounded pathetic.

"He didn't leave *you*. He left because he didn't want you to get hurt," Lyle said. "He thought he could save you."

"Go find him, Damien," Gruff suggested. "Then you can spank his ass and remind him what it means to be your boy."

Damien nodded and got to his feet. His boy was going to have a glowing butt by the time Damien worked out his fear.

"I'll come with you and search the buildings," Gruff said.

Lyle nodded. "I'll stay here in case Vinny comes back." At Gruff's worried look, he said "Jake and Alec are here. I'll be fine."

Gruff enfolded Lyle in his arms and hugged him. Damien looked away, a sour taste of jealousy in his mouth.

By the time Damien reached the stables, Thunder was saddled, Harry leading him out. The horse fidgeted restlessly until he saw Damien, who patted his strong neck. Then Damien swung his leg over Thunder's back.

Harry handed over the reins to Damien with obvious relief. "Go find him."

Damien rode out, aware the ground was slippery, frustrated by the careful pace they had to set, but he wouldn't risk Thunder too. He had no idea where to start. Where would Vinny go? If he was really trying to get away, he'd head down the mountain road to the town, not up to the deserted theme park. Nodding to himself, Damien headed for the road.

Thunder picked his way down the mountain road. Damien cursed himself. He should have taken the pick-up. It would have been quicker. But then suddenly, he caught a flash of red further down the mountain. Vinny's old coat! The relief took his breath away, and then suddenly he could breathe again as if the knot inside him had been released.

Damien picked up the pace and finally rounding a corner, he saw his Vinny, his head down, trudging down the road.

Damien rode toward him and just as Vinny realized there was someone behind him, he leaned forward, sweeping Vinny off his feet and onto the back of Thunder. Damien enfolded Vinny into his arms and pressed Vinny as tight as he could against his body.

Vinny squeaked and struggled until he realized who it was. "Daddy—" he gasped.

"No, don't speak. Not yet."

Vinny flinched and subsided against him.

They made the slow journey back to the cabin in silence, Thunder's shoes clip-clopping on the road. The only other sound Damien could hear was the rushing of blood in his ears as his heart thumped in a furious rhythm.

Damien couldn't hold a conversation, not yet. He was furious at Vinny putting himself in danger. And he still hadn't gotten over the fear that clutched his heart when he realized Vinny wasn't in the cabin.

He could feel Vinny shaking. He wasn't sure whether that was from running away, being found, being on top of Thunder, or fear of being punished. Probably a mixture of all of them. Damien was sure he was shaking too.

They reached the cabin and rode around to the old barn. Damien slid off Thunder's back, then held up his arms to lift Vinny to the ground.

Harry appeared from the barn. "I'll take care of Thunder." His expression was stern as he looked at Vinny who quaked a little. Good. Vinny needed to understand he'd scared everyone.

Damien led his boy to the kitchen door. He wasn't surprised to find Gruff and Lyle gathered in the kitchen. Their relief at seeing Vinny was palpable. The others had to still be searching for Vinny.

He stripped off Vinny's outerwear and pushed him down on the seat to unlace his boots. Then he did the same for himself.

Rexy scampered over to them, stopping in confusion as both Daddies ignored him. Gruff came over to scoop up the puppy and pet him. He wasn't happy but he quit whining and wriggling and trying to get to Vinny.

"We're going upstairs," Damien said. "We need to be alone."

Gruff nodded. "I'll let the others know."

They left the kitchen, Damien's hand wrapped around his bicep, but Damien paused when he heard someone calling his name. He gritted his teeth, annoyed at being interrupted when he was focused on his boy. Lyle hurried over, despite Gruff calling him back. The fact that Lyle ignored Gruff—and Lyle never ignored his Daddy—to talk to Damien was the reason Damien stopped.

"Stay there," he said to Vinny.

He took a step away from Vinny, who sagged as if his legs could barely carry him. Damien made sure he could reach out and grab him if necessary.

Lyle stood on tiptoe, and Damien bent his head to listen to him.

"Go easy on him." Lyle made sure Vinny couldn't hear him. Damien was about to point out it was none of Lyle's business how he treated his boy, when Lyle whispered again. "He's been badly beaten so many times."

The knowledge was a dash of iced water in the face of Damien's anger. He knew his boy had been beaten. He'd felt the scars beneath his fingertips. But still he'd been ready to go to bedroom and whale on Vinny's ass.

Damien nodded at Lyle. "Understood. Thank you."

He wrapped his hand around Vinny's bicep, and they went up the stairs. At the top Vinny headed for his small bedroom.

"Where are you going?" Damien asked harshly.

"I've been bad," Vinny gave a wretched sob. "I should be punished."

"In my room," Damien ordered.

He wasn't letting Vinny out of his sight. Not for a single second. He shepherded Vinny into Damien's bedroom. But before Damien could say a word, Vinny went to his knees before Damien, tears streaming down his dirty cheeks.

"Please don't use the tawse or cane, Daddy. Please don't hurt me. I'll be good, I promise. Please don't beat me." He didn't stop begging until Damien laid a hand on his head and threaded his fingers through Vinny's hair, soothing his crying boy.

Damien hunkered down beside Vinny. "I'm not going to hit you, my boy. I won't spank you."

Vinny looked at him, tears still dripping down his cheeks. "But you have to punish me for running away."

"I do," Damien agreed. "But there's more to

discipline than beating someone."

Damien rubbed soothing circles on Vinny's back. When Vinny had calmed down, he said, "You're going to stand in that corner with your back to me for fifteen minutes, then we're going to talk about what happened and why you ran away."

Vinny didn't move. He stared at Damien open-mouthed. "Is that all?"

Damien raised an eyebrow. "Do I need to repeat myself?"

"No." Vinny stood and hurried over to the corner and put his nose to the wall.

Damien rose and strode over to sit in the large chair. He set a timer on his phone. He knew Vinny would think this was easy punishment compared to a beating. But hopefully a little time would show him just how wrong he was.

Vinny

A tear trickled down Vinny's nose. He wiped it away. Another one followed its path. He stood sobbing quietly while his Daddy ignored him. He hated crying so much but he felt so alone.

Now he was facing the wall and he couldn't see Damien, could barely hear him except for the occasional squeak of the chair. He hated not being able to see his Daddy. He tried to move to see at least part of Damien, but he received a sharp, "Boy." He shuffled miserably back into place.

The longer he stood in the corner, the more he loathed it. He'd expected a spanking at least.

Vinny guessed Lyle had asked him not to do that. Lyle was always trying to protect him. But the spanking would have been over quicker. Fifteen minutes felt like an eternity and his legs ached. He wanted to sit down. He wanted to be in his Daddy's arms.

The alarm made him jump.

"You can come here, boy."

Vinny turned around. Damien held out his arms and Vinny rushed into them, and Damien hauled him into his lap. Vinny buried his face in Damien's neck and burst into fresh noisy sobbing. Damien threaded his fingers through Vinny's hair, rocked him, and crooned comforting nothings in his ear.

"I'm sorry. So sorry. I didn't mean to scare you," Vinny mumbled into Damien's neck.

"I know. You thought you were doing the right thing. But leaving me is never the right thing, Vinny. I thought I'd lost you and I was so scared. I remember Lyle being kidnapped. I couldn't believe that had happened again. I was so relieved when I saw you on the road."

"And angry," Vinny said in a quiet voice.

"Yes, I was angry," Damien admitted, and held him closer. "But being angry with you doesn't mean I stopped loving you. You are my boy and I'll always protect you."

Vinny curled his fingers in Damien's shirt. "But what if they keep coming for me, Daddy?"

Damien kissed his temple. "I don't think they will. But you know Alec and Jake are liaising with other agencies to make sure you're safe. They have to tell you there is a danger, but we're the big bad Brenner boys. We'll keep you safe."

Vinny leaned against him, desperately wanting to believe him, but he'd heard Jake and Alec talk. He'd seen the fear in Matt's eyes when he thought he wasn't being watched. The danger wasn't over. But Vinny could be on the run, alone in the world, or he could trust his Daddy to take care of him. Not every boy was lucky enough to have a Daddy and six other Daddy Bears to take care of them. Perhaps he could ask one of the brothers to protect Matt. He was so scared. Vinny let the gentle rise and fall of Damien's chest soothe him as Damien rocked him.

Darkness fell in the room as night drew in, but neither of them felt the urge to move. Lyle had knocked on the door to say dinner was ready if they wanted it and went away without waiting for an answer. Vinny wanted to stay where he was, cuddled in Damien's arms for the rest of the night. He offered Damien a blowjob, but Damien sighed and chuckled.

"I can think of nothing I'd like more than your sweet mouth around my cock, but I think we need to eat and make nice with Rexy. He must be wondering where you are."

Vinny felt ashamed for not thinking of his puppy. He climbed off Damien's lap and stretched his back. "I rode on your horse."

"You did. How did you feel?"

"Very high off the ground," Vinny said. "I was glad you were holding me."

Vinny didn't think he was ever going to like

being on the back of a horse, certainly not one as big as Thunder.

"I'll always hold you," Damien promised and held out his hand.

Vinny clung onto it tightly, thinking of boys who had disappeared, who weren't as lucky as him.

In the kitchen the family, except Alec and Jake who were nowhere to be seen, had already eaten, empty plates in front of them.

"'Bout time," PJ grumbled. "I was gonna eat your food."

"No, you weren't," Lyle said firmly. "I told you that food was for Damien and Vinny."

PJ gave him the side-eye. "I preferred you when you were all sweet and quiet."

"And I preferred you when you were hangdog and apologetic," Lyle shot back.

Vinny's jaw dropped, but everyone else burst out laughing, including PJ who didn't seem to take offense.

Gruff wrapped his arm around Lyle's neck and pulled him in for a hug. "I love my feisty boy."

Lyle grumbled something only Gruff could hear and he burst out laughing again.

Vinny glanced over to the puppy's bed, but it was empty. "Where's Rexy?"

"I had him for a while," Gruff said, "but then he wanted to go outside. I don't remember him coming back, but I left the door slightly open for him to come back in by himself."

"We'll go find him," Damien said easily. "We discovered yesterday what a pain he is when he's bouncing around in the snow. He'll never want to come back in."

Vinny nodded, but he was a bit concerned at his disappearance. Rexy was too young to be left outside in the snow by himself. Once they found his puppy, he would be having a chat with Gruff about not taking care of Rexy.

As if Gruff read Vinny's thoughts, he said, "I'm sorry, Vinny. I got distracted. I didn't mean to ignore Rexy."

"It was my fault Griff was distracted," Lyle said, biting his bottom lip. From the pink color on his cheeks, it wasn't hard to guess what the distraction was.

Damien led him out of the kitchen, and they put on boots and jackets as it was too cold to go out without them. The temperature had dropped considerably since they'd returned home. Damien picked up a flashlight and they went out into the crisp winter air to hunt for Rexy.

"Hey," Damien murmured. "Don't worry, little one. We'll find your pup. You know he's probably been running around in circles for a while."

"He's a baby. It's my job to look after him," Vinny insisted. "He needs me. I couldn't bear it if I lost him."

"You should take better care of him then. But you always were irresponsible."

Vinny stiffened at the familiar cold tone coming from the trees. He heard a yelp.

Rexy!

"Oh no," he whispered.

"You know who it is?" Damien demanded.

"He knows me very well," a male voice, the slither in his voice making Vinny's blood run cold.

Out of the darkness of the trees, a man dressed in a long green coat and a black hat emerged, holding a wriggling Rexy with some difficulty.

"You failed again, Vinny. It's time you were punished."

Chapter 8

Damien

"Oh no. Oh no. Oh no." Vinny clutched at Damien. "He's got my Rexy."

The puppy squealed loudly as the green coat squeezed him. It was easy to see Rexy was terrified. He wriggled and writhed but he couldn't break free of the green coat's vice-like grip.

Harry emerged from the trees, but he stopped when Damien held up his hand.

Vinny shuddered in Damien's arms, tears running down his face. "He's gonna hurt Rexy."

"Put the dog down," Damien ordered.

The green coat sneered at him as Rexy squealed again. "Make me."

Damien could see the fear and confusion in Rexy's eyes. If this asshole killed Vinny's puppy, he would tear him limb from limb. No one hurt an animal and lived to tell the tale.

They were at three points of a triangle. The green coat holding the struggling puppy, Harry, and Damien and Vinny.

"What are you doing here, Flowers?" Damien demanded.

But Flowers ignored him. All his attention was

focused on Vinny. Damien might not have existed.

Damien looked at Harry who gave a brief nod. If Flowers was only focused on Vinny that might work in their favor.

"Vinny," the green coat purred, ignoring the puppy.

He was about six feet tall, with tanned skin and ice-blue eyes. Under any other circumstance, Damien would have found him attractive, but the evil expression in the green coat's eyes and sneer on his lips, made Damien's blood run cold.

"What do you want, Flowers?" Vinny snapped.

Flowers. What an ironic name for an evil man, Damien thought. For a handsome man, Flowers looked demonic in the green coat and black hat, with black boots and gloves. He wasn't that old, maybe mid-twenties, and Damien remembered the green coats were once boys like Vinny.

Flowers tsked. "Sir. You call me sir, remember? Have you forgotten already?"

"You're not in charge of me, Flowers."

"I beg to differ, Vinny, but good to see you again. You're looking well. Have they been spoiling you?"

Damien did not like the way this man ran his lascivious gaze up and down Vinny's body.

Neither did Vinny by the way he shivered. "At least they're not beating me every day."

"You know what they say. Spare the rod and spoil the child. And you always were a naughty boy, Vinny. I loved spanking your bare ass." The man damn near licked his lips.

Damien held Vinny close to his chest and swore to himself he would never spank Vinny. Not even suggest it as something fun. It didn't take an expert to realize this guy was a sadist. From the evil look in his eyes, it was clear he'd enjoyed inflicting pain on the boys.

"It's all right, boy," Damien murmured in Vinny's ear. "I've got you. You're mine."

Maybe Vinny didn't want to be claimed by another possessive asshole, but by the way Vinny hung onto him, maybe he did.

"I'm eighteen now. You can't take me or disappear me," Vinny said.

Flowers chuckled. "You really think reaching eighteen makes any difference to me? Once you're a Kingdom boy, we can take you any time. We own you until you're dead."

"That's not true," Vinny said. "You threw us out on our eighteenth birthday. You made us disappear. We died in the woods."

"Unless we claimed you."

Damien noticed Flowers didn't deny it. But it did make him wonder if boys had escaped their fate. It was something he'd have to discuss with Jake and Alec. The thought of Vinny being in danger for the rest of his life made his blood run cold.

"And I was all ready to make you mine. I like naughty boys. I was ready to train you. Hunter couldn't touch you once you were mine." Flowers cocked his head. "But you found someone else to give you orders, didn't you?" He tsked again. "He can't have you. You're mine."

"Never!" Vinny yelled but Flowers just shrugged. "You seem to think you have a choice. How sweet." He frowned and fixed his glare on Vinny. "Don't get above yourself, Vinny. You were never destined to be a green coat, only a whore."

"There's nothing 'only' about you, boy. You're perfect," Damien whispered, pleased when Vinny pushed back against him in response.

This monster had no idea how to treat a boy like Vinny who deserved love and nurturing, not pain and brutality.

Damien saw movement in the trees. He hoped that was his brothers staging a rescue and not more green coats. Did they want Lyle too? Gruff would be devastated if Lyle was kidnapped.

"What do you want?" he asked again, hoping to distract Flowers from staring at Vinny.

The puppy had quieted in his arms as they talked, but now Rexy yelped again as Flowers twisted him.

"Let go of my fucking dog," Vinny yelled. Damien couldn't grab Vinny in time as he launched himself at Flowers.

Flowers held the dog above his head. Damien took an indecent amount of satisfaction at the puppy peeing over Flowers's hat and down his face.

"Shit! Shit! Fucking dog." Flowers let go of Rexy as he tried to get away from the steady stream of urine.

Everything happened so fast. Damien didn't have time to think. He pushed Vinny out of the way and leapt for the dog before it hit the ground.

He caught Rexy, but then saw Flowers grab Vinny by the arm and yank Vinny toward him.

Harry charged toward them, but Flowers produced a gun from his coat and aimed it at Vinny's head.

"You set one foot closer to me and he's dead," Flowers snapped.

Damien froze, still on the ground, holding Rexy in his arms, who thankfully had stopped urinating and was calm now he was in his Daddy Bear's arms.

Flowers grunted, obviously satisfied with their response. He tightened his arm around Vinny's bicep and Damien caught the white lines of pain around Vinny's mouth.

"Just stay calm, boy," Damien said to him as he put Rexy on the ground, and Vinny whimpered.

"How sweet." Flowers jammed the butt of the gun against Vinny's temple. "But he's not your boy now. He's mine and you won't see him again."

"BRENNERS!"

"Catch him!"

Unlike Flowers, Damien knew exactly what was about to happen. Flowers had been so fixated on Damien and Harry, he hadn't seen PJ and Brad emerge behind him.

Suddenly Vinny and Flowers lurched forward hard. Damien grabbed Vinny and pulled him into his arms. PJ snatched the gun. Rexy, in what was certainly revenge, shot under Flowers's feet and he tripped with a yell and landed face down on the dirt.

Brad landed on Flower's back and yanked his

arms behind his back and zip-tied his wrists together.

Harry raised an eyebrow. "Should I ask why you were carrying a zip-tie?"

"You can ask," Brad said cheerfully as he dragged Flowers to his feet. "Doesn't mean to say I'm gonna answer. Ugh. This guy stinks."

Blood dripped from Flowers's nose. No one bothered to check him out.

Damien held Vinny against his chest. His boy was shaking violently. Damien scooped Rexy up and handed him to Vinny to give him something to focus on. Then he held them both. "It's okay. It's okay, my sweet boys. You're safe. I'll never let you go again." He looked over Vinny's head at his brothers. "Is Lyle safe."

"Gruff's with him and ready to tear apart any who comes near," PJ said. "Alec and Jake are searching the grounds for intruders."

"The sheriff is on his way."

Damien grunted. The previous sheriff had been in the payroll of Kingdom Mountain Theme Park and had known what was happening to the boys. There was an acting sheriff in place. He'd yet to prove himself one way or the other.

He narrowed his eyes at Flowers. "Where are the other green coats?"

Flowers flinched back from the anger in Damien's eyes. "It's just me. I escaped from custody."

"Escaped or was helped?" Damien demanded.

The silence was answer enough. There were still traitors among the cops.

Alec and Jake jogged up to them. Damien took grim pleasure in seeing Flowers flinch at being surrounded by six huge Brenner men.

"The farm is clear," Alec said.

"He was helped to escape," Damien snarled.

Neither Alec nor Jake looked surprised. Damien had been only vaguely aware just how much more his two private investigator brothers knew about this case. They played their hands very close to their chest. But if more men were potentially going to come after his boy, Alec and Jake needed to start talking.

"The sheriff is on his way," Harry said. "Do we let him go in their custody?"

Jake nodded. "The sheriff is clean. Don't worry. Flowers will disappear from the local area. No one will be able to help him again."

Flowers flinched and Vinny hissed, "You see how you like disappearing. I hope they do the same to you as you did to us."

"You think you'll be happy here? With him?" Flowers snarled. "You're a whore for them as you were a whore for us."

The next thing Flowers was on the floor again, fresh blood running from his nose, with Damien leaning over him, his lips drawn back. Flowers tried to wriggle away but PJ put an enormous, booted foot on his bicep and pressed. Flowers screamed. No one cared.

"No one calls my boy a whore," Damien snarled. "My lovely boy is precious and will be treated as he deserves." He flexed his hand, then pulled Vinny into his arms. "Let's go home, sweetheart."

"You're turning into a caveman," PJ said.

Damien shrugged. He wasn't going to apologize for hitting the man who'd hurt his boy.

"You know the sheriff isn't going to be happy he's bleeding," Alec muttered to Jake.

Jake shrugged. "And?"

Damien led Vinny and Rexy away. And indeed. His boy was alive. That was all that mattered. And he didn't have to kill Flowers for hurting his puppy.

Vinny

Vinny shook all the way to the cabin, barely able to put one foot in front of the other. He couldn't think, couldn't get past the fear in his head. When Gruff and Lyle came to talk to him, he just buried his face in Damien's chest. He didn't want to talk to anyone, not even Lyle.

"Is he okay?" Gruff asked. He sounded worried.

"No, but he will be. He's in shock," Damien rumbled. "We're gonna rest for a while."

"Call us if you need anything," Lyle said. "And you owe a dollar for your boy."

Damien rolled his eyes and picked Vinny and Rexy up and took them upstairs. The puppy wriggled in Vinny's arms but settled at Damien's soothing command.

In their bedroom, Damien settled him and Rexy on the bed. Vinny curled around the puppy and Damien spooned around him, one large arm over him, keeping Vinny safe.

They lay in silence for a long time. Vinny

wanted to speak but he couldn't get through the white noise in his head.

"Flowers won't get you again," Damien promised, his hand over Vinny's heart.

"But he might."

"He won't. The green coats won't take you, Vinny."

"I thought I was protected here," Vinny whispered. "The cabin is my safe place. I've always felt safe in your arms."

"*I* am your safe place," Damien said. "Believe me, sweetheart, I will never let anyone take you from me."

Vinny wanted to believe his Daddy's reassurances. He really did. But now Vinny had discovered that he could be retaken at any time. He thought once he reached his eighteenth birthday, he was untouchable. Now he knew that wasn't true. He wasn't even sure Lyle knew.

"We need to tell Lyle about the danger," he said.

"I will, but not yet. There's no immediate danger and my priority is you. It will always be you."

"And Rexy," Vinny added.

"And him. Which reminds me. When Rexy's old enough, he'll get a huge steak just for himself, because he peed on Flowers."

Vinny choked out a laugh. "He was so angry."

"I know."

Vinny could hear Damien's smug smirk, even if he couldn't see it.

"Thank you for catching Rexy." Vinny sighed.

"Do you think he ought to see a vet? Flowers did hurt him."

"I bet you Harry will be knocking on the door soon to take Rexy away. He's better than any vet."

"And cheaper," Vinny said dryly.

"I see Harry's been talking to you."

"They all talk to me," Vinny admitted. "They sit down and talk to me when I'm peeling the potatoes."

"They like having someone to talk to. It can get very lonely up here. You're a good listener."

Vinny chuckled. "You mean I'm trapped with the potatoes."

"Captive audience," Damien agreed.

Vinny hadn't really thought about it until now, but at least once a day one of the brothers sat down to talk to him, even Gruff when Lyle was away from home. It was mainly to talk about Lyle because he missed him, but as Vinny was the only person who knew Lyle even better than Gruff, Vinny didn't mind talking to him about his boy. Alec and Jake didn't so much talk to him, rather interrogate him about the theme park. Harry liked talking about the horses. PJ and Brad just liked to tease him about Damien, but he'd gotten used to it by now.

The fact was he liked their company and they seemed to like him. It made him feel more like part of the family that he'd never had. Even if it was bonding over potatoes.

As if on cue, there was a gentle tap at the door and Harry said, "Is it okay to come in? I just want to check on Rexy."

The puppy had settled down to sleep, his head resting on Vinny's thigh, and seemed to be fine, but Vinny was still worried about him. Damien called out to agree and Harry came in. He rolled his eyes at the sight of the small family wrapped around each other on the bed, but it was more of a gentle tease than a nasty one.

"Why don't I take Rexy?" Harry suggested. "You guys could do with time together."

"Don't feed him too many treats," Vinny warned. "You'll only upset his stomach."

"Noted." Harry's eyes twinkled as he scooped Rexy into his arms. Rexy grumbled but he settled down because Harry soothed him.

As soon as the door closed behind him, Vinny rolled into Damien's arms, and started to cry. He'd been brave and feisty, even for his puppy, but now he was alone with his Daddy, the dam cracked, and the tears rolled down his cheeks.

Damien rocked him in his arms. "It's okay, my boy, you're safe. I promise you, you're safe."

"I don't want them to take me away again," Vinny sobbed. "They just want to hurt me."

Damien held him closer. "I am your Daddy, and no one, and I mean no one, will ever hurt you again. It's you and me against the world."

Vinny shuddered and pushed in closer to him. Damien's arms were strong and his chest broad. Vinny felt as if he could truly hide in his Daddy's arms forever. He couldn't stop crying and he remembered the number of times the green coats had told him to 'man up', usually when they were beating his ass. Damien didn't seem to care about the tears. He rocked Vinny and crooned at him, and Vinny knew he was safe.

It took a long time for the tears to subside, and he was a mess by the time he finished. As Damien gently wiped Vinny's eyes and nose, he told him he had a lifetime of tears to let out.

"Your sweater is soggy." Vinny grimaced at the mess he'd made of Damien's navy-blue sweater. "And covered in snot."

"Easily dealt with." Damien stripped off his sweater and threw it in the direction of the hamper.

Vinny's mouth went dry at the sight of Damien's strong, muscled body under the crisp, white undershirt. He reached out to run a hand down the strong muscles of Damien's arms, along the taut abs and stomach. Damien twitched a little in places. Vinny grinned. His big Daddy was ticklish. Vinny tugged at the undershirt.

"Take it off, Daddy," he begged.

Damien ripped the undershirt over his head, leaving acres of skin under soft dark hair for Vinny to explore. Damien's body was a work of art and Vinny loved every inch of it.

"You should be in a museum," he murmured, running his hands over the warm bare skin.

Gruff had shown him sculptures of male bodies in museums. None of them compared to his Daddy.

"I'd rather be in our bed with you than some dusty old museum," Damien declared. "Let me make love to you, my boy. Remind you who you belong to. Let me show you possession can come with love and kisses, not abuse and pain."

In his heart, Vinny knew that Damien wasn't like Flowers. But Damien was right. He needed to be shown it. He needed Damien buried in his body and telling him he was loved.

Vinny knelt in front of Damien, his head bowed. "Undress me, Daddy?"

It was a question, a request, not an order. And Damien nodded, bending to brush a soft kiss on Vinny's mouth.

Vinny stayed passive as Damien took his clothes off piece by piece and removed the rest of his own clothes until they were naked against each other, hard cocks leaking and sliding side-by-side. Damien's body hair was a delicious friction against Vinny's soft skin, reducing him to a bundle of nerves. Vinny's gasps captured by Damien's warm mouth against his. Nothing Damien gave him was pain. It was all love and sensation. Damien would never hurt him, he'd promised that when they'd been lying there together.

Then his Daddy prepared him and slid his thick cock inside. Because it was his Daddy and his Damien, because they were the one and the same. And Vinny never had to feel the hard thud of the tawse again. Because he was safe. Vinny was safe.

Chapter 9

Damien

Vinny passed out almost as soon as they'd finished making love, exhausted by the events of the day. Damien gently pulled out, staggered to the bathroom, and returned with a warm washcloth to clean his boy. It barely disturbed Vinny's sleep.

Damien was tired but not ready to settle. His head still felt jumbled after the encounter with Flowers. He decided to take a quick shower. He felt dirty after hitting the green coat. He knew it was in his head, but just touching the man who'd hurt his boy made him want to vomit.

He gave himself a cursory rub with the towel, then wrapped it around his waist and wandered back into the bedroom. Vinny had sprawled out in the bed, arms and legs splayed like a starfish. He also had a puppy sleeping on his belly. Someone had sneaked Rexy back into the room. Damien frowned for a moment. He didn't like the thought of anyone ogling his sleeping boy. He would have words with his brothers.

Damien dropped the damp towel and settled himself on the bed, nudging Vinny over to give him space. He caressed the puppy behind his ears. "We're going to have an issue if you sleep like this all the time."

Rexy opened one eye, yawned at him, then went back to sleep.

Vinny mumbled, "Me or Rexy?"

"Either. Both." Damien leaned over and pressed a kiss to Vinny's temple. "I love you, boy."

"Love you too, Daddy."

Vinny yawned and rolled over, dislodging the dog who grumbled, but settled between them. Damien thought about moving Rexy, but they were all comfortable, and could nap for the rest of the afternoon. They had worries to deal with but at this moment, nothing was more important than the three of them in the bed.

Hunger drove them both downstairs late that night. Damien's stomach growled like a snapping alligator. Did alligators growl? He didn't care. He just needed food to quell the ravening beast. Vinny laughed every time he heard his Daddy's belly rumble.

They agreed they'd bring the food back to bed, so they just slung on soft robes. Damien had bought a blue robe for Vinny, which matched his. As they went downstairs, Damien could hear noises from his brothers' bedrooms. It didn't take a rocket scientist to work out what Gruff and Lyle were doing.

Vinny snorted at a loud, happy shout. "I'm surprised you don't wear earmuffs. I can always hear them."

Damien grinned. "We're all gay Daddies. It's not like we haven't heard each other over the years. We know most of the boys in the area."

Vinny bit his lip, obviously not liking that answer. "Would you share me with your brothers?"

"Hell no." Damien was aghast at the idea. "I'm a one-Vinny Daddy. You never have to worry. I'll never share you with anyone. I'd kill my brothers if they laid a hand on you. I thumped PJ and he was teasing!"

Vinny gave him an oddly possessive smile. "That was the right answer."

Damien did have a history of threesomes, although never with his brothers. He'd known he was a Daddy as long as he'd known he wasn't into girls. He'd been a late starter compared to his brothers, but he'd more than made up for it. Damien didn't think now was the time to tell Vinny about the previous boys in his life. Somehow he didn't think Vinny would take it too well. That was the kind of thing that could be discussed later in their relationship, preferably when Vinny was tied up and couldn't run away.

The kitchen was empty. Damien picked up the note on the table. He recognized Harry's sprawling handwriting.

Dinner in fridge.

Rexy fed no matter what he tells you.

Flowers in custody. Alec and Jake away overnight.

"They've left dinner for us in the fridge," Damien said.

Vinny hurried over to look in the huge

refrigerator. He pulled out two covered plates. "Lyle's been cooking again. Pot roast."

Damien groaned with pleasure. He adored Lyle's pot roast. Then he saw Vinny's scowl. "I'm sorry. That wasn't meant to say your cooking isn't wonderful."

Vinny's scowl faded and he giggled. "I was teasing you. I know Lyle is a great cook. We were trained by the same boy. But I can never do pot roast like Lyle."

Damien folded his arms across his chest and raised one eyebrow. "You were yanking my chain, boy?"

He saw Vinny swallow hard and hang his head.

"I was, Daddy. I'm sorry."

Damien hummed. "You sassed me, boy. What shall I do about it?"

"You could...could...smack my bottom."

Damien saw the sudden fear in Vinny's eyes. He gathered Vinny into his arms, feeling the boy shiver. "Baby, I will never spank you. I'll keep telling you that until you believe me." He stroked Vinny's hair and held him until he calmed.

"What will you do to punish me?" Vinny asked.

"Discipline, my boy," Damien corrected. "To remind you that I'm the Daddy in charge. But never with pain."

Vinny sighed as he rubbed his cheek against Damien's robe. "I'm so lucky to have found you."

"I'm the lucky one, Vinny. I never thought I'd find a boy as perfect for me as you are," Damien said, his voice choked with emotion.

Vinny leaned back to look into his eyes. The

fear had gone. All that was left was uncertainty. "Have you quit trying to send me away or find me another Daddy?"

Damien pressed their mouths together. The soft kiss turned into something fierce. Damien slid his hand inside Vinny's robe and cupped his soft bare butt with his hands to haul him closer. He felt Vinny's hard dick leak against him, knowing his boy was as aroused as he was. By the time they pulled back, both of them panting, Vinny's eyes were glazed over with pleasure. Damien was tempted to bend his boy over the kitchen table and fuck him senseless. Vinny seemed about to launch himself at Damien when a rumble broke the silence.

Vinny giggled. "Was that you or me?"

"Me," Damien admitted, sure his cheeks were hot. He rubbed his belly. "It's been a long time since I fed the beast."

From the way it gurgled, his stomach agreed. Lunch had been a very long time ago. So much had happened since then.

"Sit down, boy. Sex can wait. I'll feed you first."

"I thought we were taking the food back to bed?" Vinny asked. "Can't we do both?"

"It's pot roast and I'm not that coordinated," Damien admitted.

"I've seen you handle an axe. Believe me, Daddy, you're perfectly coordinated."

Damien laughed as Vinny leered at him and licked his lips. This was how he loved his boy. Cheeky and sassy and without fear in his eyes.

"Me and gravy. It's always disastrous. Just ask

Alec. Besides, I want to feed you without any of my brothers here."

At some point the brothers would have to think about living apart from each other. Damien was sad at the thought, but his brothers were grown up. They didn't need him anymore. This wonderful boy in front of him did.

Vinny cupped Damien's cheek, his brow furrowed. "Why do you look sad, Daddy?"

"I'm just thinking about the future."

"And that makes you sad?"

Damien smiled and Vinny's worried expression eased. "I've spent my whole life taking care of my brothers. But they don't need me anymore."

"Because they're finding boys of their own," Vinny said.

"Yes, and because they're grown men."

Vinny smirked. "Daddy, you're all real grown."

Damien rolled his eyes. "And that's kinda sad because it's been my job, but good because now the only person I need to take care of is you. We could build our own cabin close-by."

"Just for you and me?"

Damien nodded.

Vinny's eyes went wide. "Wow. I've never lived on my own before. I only remember the dorms full of boys."

"Let's eat," Damien suggested, "and we can make plans. Sit down, boy."

Vinny furrowed his brow. "Isn't that my job? To take care of you?"

Damien shook his head. "Cooking for us as a family is one thing. But one of the joys of my life is taking care of my boys."

He could still see the uncertainty in Vinny's eyes, but that was okay. He would have a lifetime to convince him.

Vinny

Damien was right. He was hopeless with gravy. But Vinny didn't care about the few drips that landed on his chest and thighs. He sat naked on Damien's lap, hoping none of the others came down and found him like this. Only his Daddy got to see him naked. Damien had suggested his robe might be a casualty of the gravy. Rexy had weaved about their ankles in hope of tidbits, but he'd given up with a huff when he discovered his two daddies were absorbed in each other.

Vinny's bare ass was tickled by the hair on Damien's thighs, and his cock thickened every time Damien brushed the tip. His Daddy seemed to do that a lot.

"You're deliberately teasing me, Daddy," Vinny accused.

"Chew, then speak," Damien said, but his severe tone was belied by the twitch of his lips at the corners of his mouth. And there was another brush of Vinny's dick and a broad grin at Vinny's gasp.

Vinny pouted and chewed, but Damien ignored him, feeding him small spoons of food until Vinny had gotten more confident about being fed. Vinny was sure they could have eaten a lot quicker if he'd fed himself, but Damien insisted, and

Vinny didn't want to disappoint his Daddy.

It was nice to snuggle against him, listening to Damien ramble about his plans for a cabin for the two of them. Vinny could tell that Damien had given a lot of thought to what it would be like, having a home and a boy of his own. Vinny had never imagined life past eighteen. He'd never expected anyone to claim him. Had Flowers really intended to take Vinny for himself? The mere thought of the green coat made him shiver.

"Vinny, what's wrong?" Damien paused, a spoon halfway to Vinny's mouth.

"I thought about what Flowers wanted to do to me."

Damien put the spoon down and cuddled Vinny against him. "Are you scared he'll escape and come after you again?"

"No, it was you talking about our future. I never had a future before you rescued me. Now you're talking about our own home."

"And it's scary?"

"A little," Vinny admitted. He glanced up and saw the familiar look of worry in Damien's eyes. "It doesn't mean to say I don't want to be with you."

Damien brushed a kiss against Vinny's hair. "I know. And I'm not letting you go."

Vinny breathed a sigh of relief that he didn't have to have that conversation again. Why did his big, beautiful Daddy have such low self-esteem?

They finished their dinner, and maybe Rexy got one or two treats. Vinny wouldn't tell Harry. Then they stepped into the crisp night air to give

Rexy a potty break. Rexy bounced off through the snow, yipping at something only he could see.

"Maybe this wasn't such a good idea," Vinny shivered, white gusts of breath in front of him. His robe wasn't nearly thick enough to cope with the freezing mountain air. "I've gotten soft. I was used to wearing the thin uniform." Damien wrapped his arms around him, and Vinny sighed as he leaned back against Damien's solid body. "That feels good."

"You know every time I hear how you were treated, it makes me want to hunt down every green coat that's still alive, and turn them naked into the snow to disappear," Damien murmured. "Also setting wolves, coyotes, and bears on them. I think about that too."

Vinny didn't have any issue with that. He'd had more than one of those fantasies over the years. "My caveman Daddy."

"You make me like it, boy," Damien said ruefully. "I was always the calm brother, but since I met you, I would fight the world to protect you."

Vinny tilted his head to look at Damien. "You know that doesn't put me off you, don't you? No one has ever been protective of me before. Except Lyle. He tried to protect everyone."

"Now he has his own Daddy to defend him."

"He deserves it. He was always like Snow White taking care of everyone. Now he has a Prince Daddy of his own, just like I do." Vinny shivered. "Where's that damn puppy of yours. I swear he would live in the snow if we let him."

Damien snorted. "Mine? He's your pup,

remember?"

"Not when he's making me stand in the cold night air, freezing my balls off." Vinny yelped as an ice-cold hand wrapped around his balls. "What are you doing? Get off."

"I'm warming your balls for you," Damien said. "You said they were cold."

"Your hand is freezing! There's no warming here. My balls are gonna climb back inside my body. And where's the puppy?"

"Rexy's on the other side of the yard. I can see him. And my hand will warm soon," Damien purred in his ear. "See?"

Vinny grumbled under his breath, not convinced by this argument, but on the other hand, his Daddy's hand was large, and it did feel good around his nuts now it was warming up. Vinny spread his legs wider to give Damien more access.

Damien hummed in his ear. "Clever boy." He spread his fingers wider, stroking along Vinny's sensitive taint. Vinny leaned back against Damien and wrapped his arm around Damien's neck. He was hard now, and his balls were in the nice warm cocoon of Damien's hand.

"I'm going to make my boy come right here," Damien purred, "then I'm gonna carry him to bed and fuck him until the only thing he can focus on is his Daddy's cock."

"I can live with that," Vinny gasped.

"You say 'Yes. Daddy,'" Damien chided and took his hand away from Vinny's balls.

Vinny keened at the loss. "Yes, Daddy. Please,

Daddy."

"What do you want, boy."

"Your hand. Please, Daddy. I need your hand back."

"Like this?" Damien barely touched him.

"You're being mean. Daddy." Vinny covered Damien's hand with his smaller one and pressed it around his balls, taking pleasure in the extra pressure. "This feels so good."

"My boy feels so good to me," Damien assured him.

Vinny sighed in pleasure as Damien enveloped his dick in his warm hand and gave it a slow jack. Vinny's toes curled in his boots. Damien did it again, slow and languorous, and Vinny's legs threatened to give way.

"I could stand here all night doing this to you," Damien murmured. "Never letting you come until I was ready."

If it wasn't so damn cold, Vinny would be up for that. Damien was so good at reducing Vinny to a satiated mess of happiness.

Damien jacked him again and pulled a groan from Vinny that seemed to be drawn from his toes.

"But I think maybe we need a change of scene," Damien suggested. "I can hear your teeth chattering. Our bed?"

"That's a real good idea," Vinny agreed fervently. "Do you want to catch the pup. I don't think I can walk. I have this problem, you see."

"I can see this," Damien agreed, brushing the head of Vinny's cock.

Vinny gasped. "Please, Daddy, please."

Damien hummed in his ear. "Please what, baby boy?"

"Take me to bed."

Damien swept Vinny into his arms. "Rexy, here."

Vinny giggled. There was no way his naughty puppy was going to obey him. He prepared for a battle of wills.

But Rexy bounced up to them, panting happily at their feet.

Vinny's jaw dropped open. "How did you manage that?"

"He knows who's in charge," Damien said smugly, pushing the door closed with his foot.

Vinny opened his mouth to be snarky but stopped as Damien whispered in his ear. "And so do you."

Oh, he did, he so did. Vinny curled his fingers around Damien's robe. He knew exactly who was in charge.

But it wouldn't hurt to let his Daddy think he ran the show. Especially when Damien loved him so hard.

Vinny was in a deep sleep when he was disturbed by shouting. He'd woken himself by calling out so many nights, at first he wasn't sure if it was him who'd shouted. The room was pitch black compared to the bright lights of the theme park. It had taken Vinny weeks to get used to the darkness of the cabin and to be able to fall asleep without the light on. But now he was used to the dark, particularly when he was next to the safety of his Daddy.

But then it happened again.

"I'm not ugly! I'm not!"

Vinny sat up to look at the dark shadow that was Damien. But Damien snuffled, rolled over on his side away from Vinny, and started snoring. Vinny waited, just in case, but Damien didn't speak again. Vinny shook his head. He had no idea why Damien thought he was ugly. The man was very handsome, just like all the Brenner brothers. Vinny was going to have to get to the bottom of this. He settled down and spooned around Damien's body.

"I don't like girls," Damien said clearly.

Vinny snorted. "That makes two of us, Daddy."

Chapter 10

Damien

Damien rolled over onto his back, blinking sleepily at Vinny sitting cross-legged and naked on the bed, a stuffed bear which had seen better days shoved rather than cradled under one arm, as he stared at a toy car and a homemade wooden train with an intent but also exasperated look.

Damien ran a hand down Vinny's bare back. "What's the matter, my boy?"

"I'm supposed to play with these."

"You are? Who told you to play with them?"

"Lyle."

Damien knew he was still half-asleep, but this didn't make sense. "Why did Lyle tell you to play with one engine and one car and one bear, which if I'm not mistaken was mine."

"I always ask for your things," Vinny said absently, his focus still fixed on the toys.

Damien had been hoping for a snuggle with his boy, but Vinny obviously had his mind on other things. He sat up, dislodging Rexy, and picked up the train. "I used to play trains as a kid. My dad made the engines out of our wood. Most of my brothers were more into Legos."

"What are Legos?" Vinny asked.

"You don't know what Legos are?"

Vinny looked up then and saw Damien's astonished expression. "No. I've never played with toys. At least I don't think so. They made us start work at an early age. We never had playtime. I don't know what to do with these."

Damien reminded himself that Vinny wasn't anything like the boys he'd played with before. He'd been shut off from the world, working instead of having fun and playing games. Damien ached for what Vinny had lost.

"Why did Lyle give you these toys?"

"I said I didn't know how to be a boy," Vinny muttered. "He told me about play time and learning to read and write, and—"

Damien nodded, saying, "I get the picture."

"He likes playing with toys. It reminds him of when he was small, and his parents were alive."

"But you don't have those memories," Damien said quietly.

"No. I don't remember anything except sweeping and cleaning and cooking."

Damien wanted to hurt someone, but he kept his voice soft. "What do you feel when you cuddle Mister Bear?"

Vinny looked at him blankly.

Damien pointed to the toy bear.

"Oh." Vinny flushed. "I thought you meant you."

Damien's lips twitched. "Mister Bear. I've been called worse."

Vinny looked down at the bear and then at

Damien. "I like cuddling you. You're warm and sexy. I don't see the point of the bear."

"What about when you cuddle and play with Rexy?"

Vinny reached over to rub the belly of the puppy who was on his back, all four paws in the air. "Playing with Rexy is fun, and I like cuddling him."

"So maybe you like real things to play with rather than inanimate toys," Damien suggested.

"In...animal?" Vinny wrinkled his brow, obviously confused.

"Inanimate. Not real. Like the car or train. Instead of playing with toy cars, I could teach you to drive."

Vinny's eyes widened. "You'd do that? You'd teach me to drive a car?"

"Sure. Then you'd be able to go into town." Damien was painfully conscious his boy had still never left the mountain.

Vinny looked horrified. "Down the mountain road? I might drive off the edge."

"I'll make sure you get plenty of practice. We all got *real* good at driving because of that road." Damien remembered some close calls and decided not to share those stories with Vinny.

Then Vinny frowned again.

"What's wrong, Vinny?" Damien asked.

"Does this mean I'm not really a boy?"

Damien sat up, wondering where this was going. "Why do you think that?"

"If I don't like toys? Does this mean I'm not a boy? Lyle likes playing with toys."

Damien let out a relieved breath. "There are all kinds of boys, sweetheart. Some are littles like Lyle. Some like wearing diapers. Others like wearing dresses and pretty clothes."

Vinny wrinkled his nose. "I don't want to wear diapers or dresses."

"We never judge boys for their choices," Damien chided. "A Daddy's job is to nurture a boy and meet their needs."

"Sorry, Daddy. I don't mean to be rude," Vinny said, looking ashamed. "I'm still not sure what kind of boy I am."

Damien pulled Vinny into his arms.

"Ouch!" Vinny wriggled, reaching under his butt to pull out the toy car. "That hurt, Daddy."

"Sorry," Damien soothed. "Want me to kiss the ouchie better?"

"Yes, please, Daddy."

Damien let Vinny go so he could get onto his hands and knees and present Damien with his perfect butt. It was crisscrossed with white and pink scars, but still perfect. Damien's mouth went dry at the pert cheeks and his taut balls and dick.

Vinny glanced over his shoulder. "Are you going to kiss my ouchie?"

It was easy to see the red marks on his left cheek where he'd sat on the car, but Damien pressed a kiss to the right cheek.

"Is this where the ouchie is?"

Vinny giggled. "No, Daddy."

Damien kissed the base of his spine. "What about here?"

"Colder."

Oh ho. His boy liked a little game. Well, he could play too.

Another kiss. "Here?"

"Warmer!" Vinny sang.

"Here?" Damien nipped at the cheek.

"Ouch! Colder."

Damien pressed a line of kisses from Vinny's hole to his balls. Vinny sighed and pressed against his mouth.

"Any closer?" he asked.

Vinny hummed. "Down a bit."

Damien smiled against his skin. "Like here?" He sucked in the tip of Vinny's cock.

"Just like that," Vinny sighed.

Damien spread Vinny's thighs further apart so he could kiss up his shaft and balls and back to his sweet pink hole.

"Daddy!"

Someone had never been rimmed before. Damien would rectify that. He loved that he would be his boy's first everything, and last, if he had his way. Vinny would be his forever.

"Ahhhhh!" Vinny clutched at the comforter as Damien rimmed his hole.

Damien took his time, licking and rimming until Vinny was moaning, no words, just an incoherent stream of sound. He wrapped his hand around his boy's dick, so hard it had to be painful. One tug and Vinny climaxed, hips pumping furiously as white streaks flew over the comforter.

Vinny's muscles gave way and he collapsed onto the bed. Right into the wet patch, but that didn't seem to bother him from the satiated smile on his face.

Damien stroked down his back. "Did I kiss the ouchie?"

Vinny managed a hum. From his lax smile, his boy was done for a while, but Damien's own arousal needed attention. Damien looked at the long line of Vinny's back. What a lovely canvas he could use to paint his own stripes.

Damien got to his knees and jacked his cock, throwing his head back as his orgasm coiled like a snake ready to strike. Sweat drops trickled down his chest to be caught in his fur. He came with a shout, striping come over Vinny's ass until his thigh muscles shook. He was ready to collapse over Vinny's body, but he rolled to one side, not wanting to crush his boy.

"You look very pretty when you come, Daddy," Vinny said, his speech slurred.

Damien smiled. He leaned forward and kissed Vinny's cheek. "That's very sweet, but you don't have to lie."

Vinny frowned and raised his head. "I'm not lying. You are pretty, Daddy."

"How did I get so lucky with you?" Damien said, leaning forward to kiss him.

Vinny's frown didn't disappear, but he accepted the kisses.

"I think my boy needs a bath," Damien murmured as he pulled back.

"I'm covered in us," Vinny agreed, looking down at himself.

"It's a good thing I have a nice big tub just right for a Daddy and his boy."

Damien had his parents' bedroom. He hadn't wanted to take it over, but neither had his brothers, and he realized the only way for Greg to move out of the small room that was now Lyle's play room, was for him to move into the main bedroom. It had taken him a while to settle in, but in the end it had become his personal space. The advantage was the huge bathroom with a bath big enough for two.

He kissed Vinny again and went to fill the tub. On impulse he added bubbles. Vinny was almost asleep when Damien returned, and he grumbled as Damien picked him up.

"You'll feel better once I bathe you."

"You always make me feel better," Vinny said sleepily.

Damien settled them both in the water, Vinny cradled against him. His boy gave a sleepy giggle at the bubbles. Damien had fun toys but after their conversation and Vinny's frustration, he decided not to play with them this time. Vinny seemed content just to be cuddled in the hot scented water.

"I dreamed about this," Damien whispered to Vinny.

"A bath?"

"Bathing my boy. And feeding him and cuddling him."

"I never had that," Vinny said sadly.

Damien held Vinny closer. "You do now. And for the rest of your life."

"Can I be a boy even when I'm old?"

"I've known boys in their seventies. It's not

about the age, it's about who you are."

"Wow." Vinny sounded shocked.

Damien grinned as he thought of cuddling a gray-haired Vinny on his lap.

Bring it on!

Vinny

Vinny still had to peel the potatoes. Piles and piles of potatoes. Lyle had vanished with Alec and Jake for a meeting, and Damien...well, Vinny had no clue what Damien was doing other than he'd gone into town with Brad and would be back in time for dinner.

Vinny wasn't on his own though. Harry and Gruff had popped in to keep him company, and Vinny had to admit the mindless task of peeling the potatoes had been exactly what he needed after the drama of the past few days.

Rexy circled around his feet, growling, and using his toes as toys. His puppy had a sharp nip, but a stern "No!" and the dog backed off, at least for five minutes.

He'd had a stew cooking in the Crockpot and by the time dinner arrived, Vinny was hungry and ready for food and a quiet evening with his Daddy.

Damien was back, although curiously tight-lipped about what he'd been doing. All the brothers were there, with Matt as a guest. He spent most of the meal staring longingly at Alec. Vinny wondered if Matt realized Alec spent just as much time staring at him.

The drama started after Vinny served up the apple pie.

"We ought to get a photo of all of us," Gruff said. "I looked at Mom's box of photos. We haven't had a photo of us since I was a kid and most of them, I'm not in."

"You weren't born, dipshit," PJ said.

"Dollar," Brad said.

PJ sighed but he stuffed a dollar into the jar.

"Time for a new one then."

"I could take it after dinner," Matt suggested.

"We should be careful. If Damien's in it, he could crack the lens."

Vinny, who'd been talking to Harry about how to train Rexy, felt Damien's immediate flinch. He launched himself to his feet, his fists clenched and eyes flashing at PJ. "Don't you dare say that about my beautiful Daddy!"

PJ's jaw dropped open and the table went silent.

"It's all right," Damien said. "I'm used to it. I...uh...need to check on something."

It was so obvious he was hurt and needed to hide. Lyle stood up to go after him, but Vinny wasn't having that.

"Damien is my Daddy and I'm the only one who's gonna take care of him. Got it?" he snarled.

Lyle nodded, his eyes wide. Vinny looked around the table at each brother. They all seemed shell-shocked.

"Why do you make fun of his looks?" he demanded.

"Uh...it was his nickname," Brad said. "He started it. Called himself the ugly duckling. It was nothing more than a joke."

"It may have been a family joke, but it stops now. Mocking Damien's looks ends here and now. I mean it. You've no idea of the effect it's had on him."

He fixed each brother with a glare, making sure he got a nod from each of them.

"I'm sorry," PJ said. "I never realized it bothered him."

"Now you do, and it's not me you should be apologizing to. I'm going to find him. Come on, Rexy."

Vinny tugged on his boots. He hadn't got a clue where to start looking for Damien. He looked up to see Harry standing in the kitchen doorway.

"I'd try the old barn first," Harry suggested. "Damien often goes to talk to the horses when he's upset."

Vinny gave a curt nod. "Thanks. I'll try there."

"We didn't know he hated it," Harry said.

"Maybe you weren't looking," Vinny snapped as he stomped out of the cabin, Rexy at his heels.

Vinny was relieved to find Damien exactly where Harry said he would be, resting his head against Thunder's strong neck. From where Vinny stood, the temperamental stallion seemed to curl around Damien as if to comfort him. Damien didn't see Vinny immediately. He looked crushed. A simple joke had crushed him. Vinny wasn't going to let this go any further. Vinny stepped toward the stall, but not close enough to upset Thunder. But the horse shifted restlessly and Damien raised his head. He didn't look surprised to see Vinny, but his smile was strained.

"I'm sorry, boy. I ruined dinner."

"I don't give a fuck about dinner," Vinny said clearly.

Vinny was sure Damien's lips twitched, but being Damien, he scowled.

"Language."

Vinny opened his mouth to say he didn't give a toss about his language either, but Damien gave him a long, steady look and Vinny shut his mouth.

"Wise choice," Damien said.

Vinny sighed. "Talk to me, Daddy. Tell me why you're so convinced you're ugly."

"Look at me," Damien muttered.

"I do. All the time."

Damien smiled at Vinny's prompt response. "I guess you do."

"And you know that I love staring at you. But you seem to think you're ugly and I don't know why."

Damien sighed. "My mom thought I was."

Vinny had the sudden feeling quicksand was in front of him and if he didn't tread very carefully, he'd be sucked down and never seen again. "Your mom told you that you were ugly?"

All the brothers had talked about their parents to Vinny in their potato peeling visits. Without exception they'd talked about how kind their mom had been and how much she loved them, including Damien. Vinny had thought Damien and his mom had a special bond. But to tell a son he was ugly was a cruelty Vinny hadn't expected.

"Mom was chatting to a neighbor. They didn't

know I was listening."

"How old were you?"

"Twelve. Gruff had just been born."

"So your mom had just given birth."

"That's what I just said," Damien muttered, a touch irritably.

Vinny nodded. His mom must have been tired with six boys and a new baby. "So what did she say?"

"This is old news, Vinny. It's doesn't matter."

"Tell me," Vinny insisted.

"Old Mrs. Viner said 'Well, he has to be good for something. He's never going to be a looker. Your boys certainly improved the more you had. This one is as cute as a button.'" Damien repeated the words in a monotone fashion.

It didn't matter? Those words had obviously been seared into Damien's brain for nearly thirty years.

"And what did your mom say?"

"She said I was a young and growing lad. I had time to improve."

Ouch. That had to have cut deep for a boy on the verge of manhood. His mom had probably said it to shut up an annoying neighbor, never realizing her son had just heard her dismiss his looks.

"The neighbor said girls wouldn't be interested in me," Damien muttered.

And that explained the previous night.

"Did your mom say anything else, Daddy?"

"I had a kind heart and I'd never work anywhere except the farm." Damien gave a bitter laugh. "She was right about that."

Vinny ached for the boy who'd just heard his future decided for him.

He watched Damien sweep a brush over Thunder's coat. "Daddy, is Thunder finished."

Damien stared at the brush as if he wasn't sure how it had gotten into his hand. "I guess so."

"Then come with me."

"Where are we going?" Damien asked.

"To our bedroom. I want to show you something."

Vinny had something very important to show his Daddy and it couldn't wait any longer.

They walked back to the cabin. Before they'd gotten through the door, Damien was surrounded by his brothers. Vinny stood back and watched them crowd and jostle him, hugging him one by one.

"I'm sorry, Damien." PJ pulled a face as he stepped back. "I keep saying that. But I am sorry. You're my big brother. You helped bring me up. I never want to hurt you."

He hugged Damien again and stepped back for Harry to take his turn.

"You need to listen to your boy, okay?" Harry whispered in Damien's ear. "Let him tell you the truth." Harry caught Vinny's eye and winked. Then he stepped back to let the next brother in.

Finally Vinny decided he'd had enough. "I'm taking my Daddy upstairs."

"Don't scare the dog," Jake suggested. "We could keep him down here until you're...finished."

Vinny shook his head. "He's coming with us.

He'll be a good boy, won't you, Rexy?"

The pup yipped in agreement.

In their bedroom, Vinny settled the puppy in his own bed, and turned to face Damien who wore a slightly bemused look.

"Daddy, would you undress me?" He didn't want to change their roles. Damien was his Daddy and he loved that.

Damien stepped forward and slowly undid each button of Vinny's shirt, exposing his white undershirt. Then he slipped it off his shoulders. Damien tugged up the undershirt, making sure his warm hands got over Vinny's sensitive skin. By the time Damien was on his knees, pressing a soft kiss against the rigid shaft covered by soft cotton, Vinny was a bundle of sensitized nerves. But he had to keep it together to show his Daddy exactly what he thought about him.

"You get undressed too," Vinny begged, tugging Damien to his feet.

Damien stripped off his clothes as Vinny wriggled out of his briefs. Then they faced each other, both hard and wanting, but Vinny wasn't ready for that yet. He had a job to do.

Chapter 11

Damien

Damien wasn't entirely sure what was happening, but his boy had an agenda and it seemed simpler to go along with it. Also, they were naked, which suggested there might be an orgasm involved.

Vinny led them over to the mirror. "Hold me, Daddy," he begged.

He pressed his back against Damien's chest and Damien wrapped his arms around him, Damien's hard cock trapped between them. Damien was tall enough to rest his chin on Vinny's head. He knew Vinny had always mourned his lack of height, but at this moment, it was perfect. Damien thought about jacking Vinny off in front of the mirror. Was this what Vinny wanted?

"When I first met you, I was scared of you," Vinny admitted.

Maybe not a hand job then.

"I know," Damien said, dragging his mind away from sex and remembering how sad he'd felt when he realized he scared the boy.

Vinny pressed a kiss into Damien's large bicep. "But I soon realized you were my hero, my protector. You were there when I had nightmares. You protected me when I was scared. I'd never had anyone who cared about me before."

"I was trying to be your parent," Damien admitted ruefully.

"I need a Daddy, not a parent," Vinny chided.

"I'm old enough to be your father."

Vinny glowered at him. "Do you think I care about the age gap between us? You're perfect for me."

Damien pushed aside his doubts and kissed the top of Vinny's head. "And you're perfect for me." The moment he'd seen the frightened boy, he'd known he wanted to take care of the boy for the rest of his life.

"So…" Vinny took a deep breath and Damien tensed, not sure what was coming next. "You think you're the ugly duckling of the family and I'm telling you that's crap…wrong."

Damien let the curse word slide without mentioning the dollar—this time. He was more interested in what Vinny was trying to say to him.

"Look at you," Vinny continued. "You have a strong face. You're not pretty. But you're a very handsome Daddy."

Damien shook his head and gave Vinny's reflection a wry smile. "I know what you're trying to do, and thank you, but I know I'm not handsome. I'm lucky not to break the mirror."

Vinny stamped his foot, his expression cross. "What do I have to do to show you what a handsome bear you are? You're not that gawky teenager, Daddy. Look at yourself."

He stepped out of Damien's arms and pushed him in front of the mirror, holding onto his arm in case he was worried his lover was about to bolt. Being faced with confronting his looks, Damien was ready to run away. Vinny's instincts were probably correct.

"I know what I look like," Damien pointed out.

"No, you don't. Because if you did, you wouldn't have this stupid idea you're ugly."

Damien took a long look at himself in the mirror, seeing himself as he always did. Severe face, crazy wild beard, good hair going a bit gray at the temples, lines around his eyes now. "I look cold and severe."

"Stern, maybe," Vinny allowed, "but then you smile and your whole face lights up."

Damien couldn't help his grin just at the thought.

"Just like that," Vinny agreed with his own smile.

"I've got a big nose," Damien pointed out.

"Aquiline," Vinny said, running his finger down Damien's nose.

For a kid who'd had no formal education, where had Vinny learned that word?

"Big chin."

"A strong jaw and a soft, lush beard." Vinny cupped Damien's jaw, stroking his beard.

"Thin lips." He'd always wanted a full mouth.

"Strong mouth, just right to kiss me," Vinny said, standing on tiptoe for a kiss.

"Small eyes," Damien continued, somewhat breathless as the kiss had gotten heated.

"Big eyes, the color of a clear sky," Vinny contradicted.

"Huge and hairy."

Vinny licked his lips and ran his fingers through Damien's chest hair. "Perfect," he purred.

Damien didn't have an issue with the rest of his body, but it was nice to know someone was turned on by it. Judging by Vinny's stiff cock, he had no issues with Damien's body.

"You don't see me as I really am," Damien said. He was flattered by Vinny's earnest attempts to make him feel better, but really, it was unnecessary.

"I see you as the world sees you, Daddy. Not as you see yourself in here." Vinny tapped Damien's forehead.

Damien sighed and wrapped his arms around Vinny, pleased that Vinny subsided against him. "Thank you for trying to make me feel better, my boy. But you've got thirty years of low self-esteem to deal with. You're not going to overcome it in one session. I'll live with a cold face and a kind heart."

"You're not cold. Not to me. Not to your family." Vinny placed a hand over Damien's heart. "That kind heart shows in your handsome face."

"I don't know what to say."

He stared at Vinny's reflection in the mirror. Vinny beamed at him and of course Damien smiled back. He blinked. His whole face changed with that smile. The stern face vanished and in its place was a happy, handsome man.

"See," Vinny murmured, laying one hand on

Damien's belly and the other on his lower back.

"I see."

And for the first time, Damien really did see the man that Vinny had tried to show him. "I'm not an ugly duckling, Mrs. Viner."

"Your neighbor was just being horrid. You're never allowed to call yourself an ugly duckling again. It's banned," Vinny insisted.

Damien raised an eyebrow. "Oh? You give the orders do you?"

Vinny nodded. "When it comes to looking after my Daddy, I do."

"Did you scare my brothers?"

"Maybe a little." Vinny smirked at him.

Damien returned the smirk, but inside he'd melted into a gooey puddle. For the first time someone had his back.

"You think I'm a swan now?" he teased.

Vinny's expression sobered. "You've always been a swan, Daddy. You just needed to see it."

Damien had had enough of looking in the mirror. He turned away and pulled Vinny into his arms. "The only thing I need is to take care of you for the rest of my life."

Vinny

Vinny sighed at the knock on the door. He wasn't ready to be disturbed from his boy-time. He'd been sitting on Damien's lap for an hour in the big chair in what had been his bedroom when he first moved to the house. Damien had intended to teach him to read, using another fairy tale, but they'd spent most of the time sitting in silence, with Damien stroking his hair.

"Yeah?" Damien called out, sounding irritated.

Gruff poked his head around the door. "Sorry, guys. Jake and Alec want to talk as a family before they leave."

Damien huffed but he nodded. "We'll be down." He patted Vinny's lower back. "I'm sorry, boy. They wouldn't have disturbed us if it wasn't important. We can come back to our time afterward."

Vinny nodded. He knew it was selfish, but he wanted more boy-time. They hadn't had a chance to explore what kind of boy he was. His time with Damien away from the family was so limited. His Daddy had promised him they would work it through, but life was always intruding on their time together.

They went downstairs, holding hands as usual. The whole family sat around the table, along with Matt who seemed to spend more and more time at the cabin. Vinny didn't miss he was sitting close to Alec.

"About time," Jake muttered.

Damien glowered at him. "You disturbed my time with my boy."

To Vinny's surprise Jake apologized to them both.

"We wouldn't have bothered you, but our contacts have told us the green coats in other theme parks are going underground, and they're taking boys with them."

Vinny gasped. "They're kidnapping the boys?"

"The younger ones yes." Alec grimaced. "The older ones..."

Disappeared. Vinny got it. Matt and Lyle looked sick.

Damien put an arm around his shoulders. "I thought the authorities had closed all the theme parks."

"They have, in this area. This is a much bigger operation than we first thought and not all the authorities are taking it seriously."

"What can we do about it?" Vinny asked.

Jake exchanged a look with Alec who nodded. "We need you, Vinny. We need you and Lyle and Matt. You're the only ones who know how the theme parks operate."

"I've told you all I know," Vinny protested.

"We need you to come with us," Alec said.

"Vinny's not setting a foot outside this farm without me," Damien said flatly.

Jake rolled his eyes. "Like that's gonna happen. You guys talked about going on a road trip."

Vinny furrowed his brow. That had been a casual conversation. Something for the future.

Jake continued. "Well, it's still happening, but with stopovers."

"You mean my as-yet-unplanned road trip with my beautiful boy is now invaded by three more brothers and two boys," Damien said wryly.

"I'm not a—" Matt started.

"Yes," Alec agreed. "That's exactly it. And you don't get to decide where you're going."

"Story of my life," Damien muttered.

"No," Vinny burst out. "No! They could take me

back or hurt my Daddy. I don't...I'm scared...they could hurt me." He wrapped his arms around himself, ashamed that in that moment he could only think of himself and the pain.

Damien held him close. "They won't touch you, my boy. No one will touch you again. You're not alone anymore. You have us."

"I'm a boy with no family," Vinny said.

"No, you're not. You have a family, Vinny. Just look." Damien pointed at all the brothers sitting around the table.

They all nodded, and Lyle gave him a tender smile. Matt looked oddly wistful.

"You've been part of our family since you walked through the door," PJ boomed. "Anyone who peels that many potatoes has got to be family."

Vinny gave him a watery smile. "Thanks, PJ."

"You can be a Brenner, if you want to be," Jake assured him. "We can legally change your name. It would help to hide you from the green coats."

Vinny nodded, thinking it was a good idea. He had no attachment to his newfound last name and he desperately wanted to be a Brenner.

But Damien shook his head. "Ah, no."

Vinny stared at him, hurt forming a lump in his throat. "You don't want me to be a Brenner?"

Damien smiled at him, and the hurt eased a fraction. "Of course I do, my Vinny. I want you to become *my* Brenner boy."

Then Damien went on onc kncc in front of him.

The kitchen went silent, so quiet Vinny could

hear the *tick-tock* of the kitchen clock. Nobody said a word. Even Rexy was silent.

Vinny gasped as Damien produced a plain gold ring from his pocket and held it out in his palm.

"Vinny, would you do me the honor of becoming my husband and my boy?"

Silence. A heartbeat. Vinny was frozen in place, staring into Damien's blue gaze.

"He's waiting for an answer, dipshit," PJ muttered. Then a yelp as someone obviously elbowed him in the ribs.

Vinny ignored the byplay. The only thing he cared about was his Daddy. "Yes. Yes, I'll marry you."

Damien slipped the ring on Vinny's finger and got to his feet, drawing Vinny into his arms for a passionate, yet tender, kiss. Then they turned to look at the brothers.

Whoops, cheers, and clapping from all the Brenners, banging the table with heavy fists. Vinny had a passing thought that it was a good thing the table was so solid. Rexy barked at the top of his puppy lungs.

Lyle came around the table to hug him tight. "Congratulations, little brother."

Vinny scowled at him. "Only just your little brother." Then they grinned at each other and hugged again.

Damien pulled him back into his arms. "Are you sure you want to spend the rest of your life with me?"

Vinny tilted his head so he could press a kiss against Damien's furry chin. "I can't think of anyone else I'd want to spend my life with. You're my Daddy, my beau bear."

The End

I hope you enjoyed Damien and Vinny's happy ever after. Now it's time for Jake and Aaron's story. It's a story of unrequited love (so Aaron believes), a boy who's spent his whole life hiding, and a Daddy willing to take the time to let his boy discover his true self.

Here's a teaser for *Boy Tangled* to start.

Aaron

Aaron Yates was in hell. Absolute hell. He shouldn't even be working tonight, but one of the other bartenders was ill, and Pablo needed a cover urgently. It wasn't like Aaron couldn't do with the money. Working at the Tin Bar just about covered his rent and food, but he needed the extra shifts to survive.

Except for tonight. It was Tuesday night. Gay Daddies night at the Tin Bar. When all the Brenner boys from the Christmas tree farm on Kingdom Mountain descended on the bar, and took over the place with their bellowing voices and bushy beards. Who would believe seven huge bears of men would also turn out to be gay Daddies? The local boy population was in heaven.

Not Aaron though. He just considered the Brenners huge and annoying. He knew that was unfair and probably irrational. He didn't even mind most of them. Sure, Damien could be moody, although he was better now he'd gotten a boy of his own. The biggest one, PJ, was just an ass, although he had a ready smile for everyone, and the little twinks loved sitting on his lap or ass up, over it. No, it was Jake that was the problem.

Jake Brenner, the second to youngest brother, pushed every button Aaron had and then some. Aaron thought he was tall enough at a couple of inches under six foot. Although he was slender, he had muscles from working the bar. But Jake had at least ten inches on him and was three times the size. He had the same chestnut bushy hair and out-of-control beard most of the brothers had. He wore a blue plaid flannel shirt and jeans that had seen better days. The holes in the jeans could be distracting. Aaron dragged his gaze away from a hole too far up Jake's thigh, which showed exactly which way the bear dressed. He could see the same chestnut hair and a glimpse of bright red briefs peeking through the denim. Aaron was sure Jake had that fur all over. Aaron looked away. His penchant for furry men did not extend to Jake Brenner. At least that's what Aaron told himself.

Aaron did everything he could to avoid working Tuesday nights, even claiming that was the night he visited his granny, and he couldn't disappoint her. Pablo wasn't to know he didn't have a granny, to disappoint or otherwise. No, it was just that he wanted to avoid Jake Brenner and his revealing jeans.

It wasn't like Jake ever noticed he existed.

Aaron was just the bartender, part of the furniture. Jake spent all his time with the sweet twinks, treating them so gently just as a Daddy should. This stupidly upset Aaron, especially when Jake gave him such a hard time if he got an order wrong. It was like Jake went out of his way to find something to yell at Aaron for. And then he'd go back to his twinks and treat them with gentle tenderness that made Aaron's gut twist in bitter knots.

So yeah, he avoided Tuesdays.

But Pablo had been desperate, and Aaron needed the money. His shift had never lasted so long. The brothers were drinking, which meant they weren't playing. They never drank alcohol when they were in a scene. But it didn't stop twinks draping themselves over the unattached brothers. Especially Jake. He seemed to attract them like flies on shit. Aaron was tempted to get out the fly swatter.

It didn't help the rest of the brothers had been pleased to see Aaron, especially Damien who'd thanked Aaron for his advice. Damien had been drowning his sorrows in the bar, and Aaron had told him to go home and sort it out with his boy before he caused a fight. It seemed like Damien had taken his advice because the big man didn't stop smiling all evening, even though his boy wasn't there with him. He had never seen Damien look so happy. Jake, on the other hand, wore a frown Aaron wasn't used to, and he sunk beer after beer until he was slurring his words and unsteady on his feet. It didn't stop a beautiful young man draping himself over Jake's lap and Jake didn't push him off. Aaron gritted his teeth and tried to focus on the customers and not the Daddy of his dreams.

The brothers got louder as they got drunker. Elements of the conversation drifted over to where Aaron was tending bar. They seemed to be talking about a road trip. They were excited and worried about the trip at the same time. Aaron made sure they didn't see the look on his face. He knew most of the brothers had rarely been off the mountain. They had been born in the huge cabin halfway up Kingdom mountain, and still lived there together.

They didn't know how lucky they were. The brothers had a home and a family. Aaron had neither. He had spent the last seven years on the road, moving from job to job, never staying anywhere long enough to put down roots. This town was the longest he'd ever stayed in one place. Maybe it was time he moved on. It wasn't fair on Jake that he had the problem. Or maybe it would be easier when they left. Jake was one of the brothers going on the road trip, and Aaron would be able to breathe again when he didn't have to watch Jake love on every boy except him.

Aaron was in the middle of serving a tiny, nervous twink when there was a sudden screech, and then a roar. He looked over to see the brothers on their feet. Oh hell, what had happened in the minute he'd not been gazing at Jake?

A table was upturned, and pints of beer spilled

onto the carpet. Great, that was gonna be fun to clear up. Jake was facing off with another guy Aaron knew was also a daddy. Jake was twice the size of the other Daddy, but the guy was riled up. Jake looked wonderful, with flashing blue eyes, and bulging muscles from his clenched fists. But he wouldn't hit the other man unless the guy went for him. Then all bets were off. Aaron had been here before. He didn't miss the excited expression in the boy's eyes. Jake had put the boy behind him, to protect him as a Daddy should. What he didn't realize was that this man was the boy's Daddy. The boy had been playing him. He wanted to start a fight.

Dammit. Aaron had to cut this off before someone—Jake—spent the night behind bars or in the ER. He stormed around the bar and headed to the warring duo, holding his hand up as one of the brothers started to explain.

"I don't care who started it. You pick up the glasses and the bottles and take them over to the bar. You're all cut off for the night. I'm not barring you, but you need to get out of here."

"You can't do that," Jake spluttered, scowling at Aaron.

Aaron glowered at him. "I damn well can." He pointed at the boy. "This kid is playing you, Jake. He belongs to the other Daddy." Then Aaron turned on the guy who had started the fight. "Keep your boy and your fists under control. If he does it again both of you are barred." Aaron looked at the kid, who still looked disappointed that there hadn't been a fight. "This isn't how you treat a

Daddy. You should have more respect for him than that."

He caught Jake's speculative expression. Now what? But Jake didn't say anything.

Aaron waited for them to pick up the table and the glasses, and then shuffle out of the bar. Jake seemed...well, kind of angry but also hurt, but one of the other brothers clapped a hand on his shoulder and hustled him out of the bar before he could protest any further. Damien stopped and turned back to Aaron.

"I'm sorry about Jake. He's not normally an asshole like this, but he's had really bad news about the case we're working on. I think it's upset him."

For a second Aaron felt guilty and thought about calling them back, but it was too late. All the brothers were gone, and Aaron was left with a quiet bar and the mess to clean up.

Aaron groaned as his phone rang in his ear. He fumbled for the phone and managed to connect it before voicemail kicked in.

"Yeah?" he slurred.

"What the hell were you doing, boy?"

He got stuck on the 'boy' and it took Aaron a moment to realize it was his boss yelling at him. "Pablo? What's wrong? What did I do?"

"You threw the Brenners out of the bar."

"They were about to have a fight," Aaron said. "Jake was playing with another man's boy."

"I don't care what they were doing or who he was playing with," Pablo snapped. "You don't throw the Brenners out. Dammit, Aaron, you should know this."

Aaron was slow to catch up. He squinted at the clock and realized he'd only had four hours sleep. "Pablo..." he started.

"This is the second time you've thrown out one of the brothers," his boss roared. "These guys drink, Aaron. They pay the bills. You can't just throw them out like they're any random customer. I'm sorry, son, but that was your last shift at the Tin Bar."

Aaron sat up, Pablo's words penetrating his sleep-hazed brain. "You're firing me? For doing my job?"

"You've had it in for the Brenners ever since you arrived. I don't know what your problem is, but I can't deal with it. I'm sorry, Aaron, but we're done. Come get your pay this morning." Pablo disconnected the call.

Aaron sat up in bed and stared at the phone. He'd stopped a fight and lost his job? What the fuck? He'd lost his job because of fucking Jake Brenner. What the hell was he going to do now? He couldn't afford this room unless he worked. Yeah, the room was a shithole, but it was his. He didn't have a nice cozy cabin up in the mountains. Aaron's lip curled as he thought about who did.

Dammit, he guessed the decision about his future was made for him. Maybe it was for the best. Being near Jake Brenner was making him sour. Aaron wasn't usually like that about any man. He was an easy-going guy, ready with a smile for anyone. Now he wasn't smiling. He had two options. He could find another job in town, or he could take this as a sign and move on.

Aaron nodded to himself. It was time to go.

Two hours later he had his last pay in his pocket, an apology from Pablo but not his job back, and he was ready to leave. He'd hitchhike out of town and take the first vehicle that stopped for him. He didn't have any responsibilities and he could go where the wind took him as long as it wasn't back to *her*.

He stuck out his thumb as a truck came toward him.

Success!

The vehicle pulled up ahead of him. He jogged to the truck and opened the door.

A middle-aged, balding guy smiled at him. "Where do you want to go, son?"

"Wherever you're going as long as it's a long way from here," Jake said as he climbed in.

The trucker chuckled. "Did you get a girl pregnant? Are you running away?"

Aaron rolled his eyes. "I'm running away, but from a guy, not a girl."

He wasn't sure exactly what happened next. He heard the yell, but he didn't see the punch coming. His head cracked back, and seeing stars, he wasn't prepared for the driver to shove him out of the truck and onto the road. He hit the ice packed ground hard, the breath forced out of him from the impact.

Aaron watched the lights tear down the road and fade away. He was left dazed at the side of the road, blood dripping onto the ice, the crimson pattern almost hypnotic. It was too dangerous to remain here. He needed to find another ride. But Aaron's head ached more with every breath, and he felt sick. He'd stay where he was until he worked up the energy to move.

Want to find out who saves Aaron? Read *Boy Tangled*, the next in the Bearytales series.

Also by Sue Brown

STANDALONE books

Summer's Dawn | Summer's Song | A Tale Told in Darkness | A Cock in the Window | In-Decision | The Backpack | The Clumsy Santa | Mr Plum | Chance to Be King | Made for Aaron | Final Admission | The Layered Mask | The Next Call | The Night Porter | Light of Day | The Sky Is Dead | Nothing Ever Happens | Stolen Dreams | Waiting | Prey Time | Louis Hates Valentines Day | Racing Raindrops | The Fireman's Pole Falling for Ramos | Last Place at the Chalet | Still Loving You

JT'S BAR series

His Shield | His Guardian | His Warrior | His Valentine | His Protector | His Sentinel | His Defender

BIKER DADDY BODYGUARDS

Hold Firm | Hold Close | Hold Safe | Hold Tight | Biker Daddy Bodyguards Boxset

DARKER DADDY BODYGUARDS

Dark Heart | Dark Secret | Dark Haven | Dark

Angel

BEARYTALES IN THE WOOD
Snow Twink | Beau Bear | Boy Tangled | Jack's
Giant | Boy Riding | Beauty & the Bear | Bear in
Boots

ANGEL SECURITIES series
Morning My Angel | Goodnight My Angel | Hello
My Angel | Angel Securities Boxset

LYON ROAD VETS series
Hairy Harry's Car Seat | Bob, the Destroyer of
Leads | Hazel Takes Over | Stormin' Norman |
Lyon Road Vets Boxset

DATING MR, RIGHT series
Speed Dating the Boss | Secretly Dating the
Lionman | Slow Dating the Detective Dating Mr.
Right Boxset

WITH A KICK series (with Clare London)
Hissed as a Newt | Bells and Balls

FRANKIE'S series
Frankie & Al | Ed & Marchant | Anthony & Leo |

Jordan & Rhys |

THE ISLE series
The Isle of... Where? | Isle of Wishes | Isle of
Waves | Isle of Waiting Island Doctor | Island
Counselor |Island Detective | Isle Series Boxset

SKANDIK & OWENS series
A Body in his Bed

MORNING REPORT series
Morning Report | Complete Faith | Go-to Guy |
Luke's Present | Letters From a Cowboy | Morning
Report Boxset

MULTI-AUTHOR
A Little Christmas! Danny
My Christmas Nemesis in Kind Hearts at
Christmas
Trickle of Blood in Gothika: Fang

About Sue Brown

Sue Brown is a Londoner with a dream to live on a small island. Coffee fuels her addiction for writing romance with hot guys loving each other, and her Adorkadog snores in harmony as she creates.

Come over and talk to Sue at:
Newsletter: http://bit.ly/SueBrownNews
Bookbub: https://www.bookbub.com/profile/sue-brown
Website: http://www.suebrownstories.com/
Facebook group:
https://www.facebook.com/SueBrownsStories/
Tiktok: https://www.tiktok.com/@suebrownstories
Email: sue@suebrownstories.com

Printed in Great Britain
by Amazon

43267444R00088